Nine Rabbits

Nine Rabbits
Virginia Zaharieva

Translated by Angela Rodel

Black Balloon Publishing
New York

FIC
ZAHARIEVA

Published by Black Balloon Publishing
blackballoonpublishing.com

First published in English by Istros Books

ISBN: 978-1-936787-13-5

Black Balloon Publishing titles are distributed to the trade by
Consortium Book Sales and Distribution
Phone: 800-283-3572 / SAN 631-760X

Library of Congress Control Number: 2013953125

With support from:

Elizabeth Kostova
FOUNDATION *for*
CREATIVE WRITING

Designed and composed by Kyle G. Hunter
Cover photograph of the author as a child by Svetlozar Zahariev
Printed in the United States of America

9 8 7 6 5 4 3 2 1

I thank my parents for giving me the most precious gift—life in this body.

I thank Angela Rodel for her devotion to this text and for the wonderful translation.

I thank the Elizabeth Kostova Foundation for their support for the English edition of this book.

I dedicate this book to Christo.

Contents

PART ONE

Dresses *1*

Potatoes *3*

Granny Sweetest, Granny Dearest *7*

Baked Rabbit *9*

Gnomes and Gardens *13*

Leftovers *15*

Fried Chicken *17*

Cherry Stain *20*

Dolphins and Lemon Cream *23*

Blood *25*

Tomatoes *28*

Money *35*

Yellow Roses *39*

Nettles *43*

Siemens and the Counterrevolution *50*

Exodus *53*

Salamander *55*

PART TWO

Corset *59*

Turkey *63*

Fathers and Mothers *71*

Paris *75*

Red Dress *77*

House *80*

Christos *83*

Siamese Cats in Brocade Jackets *91*

Russian Bath *95*

Photograph *112*

Osaka *114*

Journey in the Garden *120*

Mask *124*

Diary *126*

Nobody *132*

PMS *133*

Ash Rose *137*

Love *139*

Alone *140*

Wedding *144*

Symphonia globulifera *151*

Red Dress 2 *163*

The Mad Hatter *168*

Dragons *171*

Steam *174*

At 46 *175*

Deer *179*

Calligraphy *181*

Finale *186*

Part One

Dresses

I turned up in the seaside town of Nesebar—an inconvenient four-year-old grandchild. My grandmother was raising the last two of her six children, putting the finishing touches on the house, ordering the workmen around, and doing some of the construction work herself. Thank God for this, as it used up some of her monstrous energy. Otherwise who knows what would've become of me.

Klement and Maruna, the runts of the litter, were rarely at home, since they went to boarding schools in Burgas. My aunt studied agriculture, while my uncle was at the nautical school.

Whenever I disappeared for long stretches somewhere inside the house, you could bet that I was in the attic, where there were a dozen big chests full of shoes, dresses, and all sorts of accessories brought from Czechoslovakia, where the family had prospered. Grandma Nikula and Grandpa Boris—"the Czechs," as they were called—had worked in the glass factories of Bohemia between 1948 and 1958, during the most optimistic years of the Klement Gottwald regime.

Nikula's father had been a cloth trader, so she had an eye for materials and colors. In Czechoslovakia she had sewn dresses for herself and her daughters and had even managed to marry off her oldest girl in Prague at the age of eighteen.

Nikula truly did dress with taste, although she only did so now when we went to the movies or when she stumped for the Communist Party's Fatherland Front in the nearby villages.

She took me with her. Where could she leave me? I stood in front of the podium and watched her. When she got up in front of the masses, my grandmother was very beautiful and convincing. I was proud of her; she always managed to slip in something from her own heroic biography that made her speech entertaining. For example, when she was eight months pregnant with my uncle, she helped the brigades build the Hainboaz Pass in the Balkan Mountains and was a Shock-worker despite her huge belly.

Now, absorbed in building the house, she didn't have the time or occasion to parade around in her dresses. So they all belonged to me.

The attic was plastered with a mixture of sheep manure, fine straw, and dark red clay. The scent of turds and dust accompanied my odysseys through 1950s fashion in front of a large cracked mirror, illuminated by the single skylight in the roof. First, I would put on a black satin slip with lace trim. Then I would add white silk petticoats. Next came the colorful flowered dresses—tailored at the waist, flared at the bottom. They either had straps, were backless, or had plunging necklines. Trembling, I would try them on one by one. The shoes had solid heels, open backs and another little opening at the tip of the toes. I climbed up onto the high heels and was beautiful. Dolled up like this, I would spend hours enraptured by the family treasures. Once I even found a pistol. I showed it to Rufi, my friend from next door, and then hid it again in a different spot. Grandma and Grandpa fought a lot, and I was afraid that they'd end up shooting each other some evening.

I shared the attic with giant nesting seagulls who yielded their territory to me with a squawk. At that time I hadn't yet seen Hitchcock's *The Birds,* so I studied the eggs in the nest without a thought for the mother lurking outside. During some important surveillance mission, I would hear my grandma's raspy voice: "Where are you, girl? Saraaa, Pepaaa, Marunaaa, Klemooo, Ivaaan, Veraaa!" Once she finished reeling off her children's names, completely furious, she'd hit upon my name and bark, "Mandaaaa, I'mgonnatearoutyourhair, get down from there this instaaaant!" Sometimes I thought my name was I'mgonnatearoutyourhair. "How many times have I told you not to rummage around in the attic?"

Her voice echoed through the shaft leading up to the attic. It was a difficult place to climb up to. I counted on this while hiding among the chests, but sometimes she was so mad that she'd climb up the ladder, huffing and puffing. A wild chase around the rafters would ensue; "You little turd," and "Brat" were her war cries. At first it was fun, but the fun soon ended. She would beat me with whatever was at hand—a belt, a hanger, an umbrella—and then she'd collapse, exhausted, onto some heap of clothing while I quickly escaped. I would come back late, hoping she would be asleep, but she would be lurking by the door to smack me again: this time for good-night.

Potatoes

The scent of potatoes, steamed with butter, Czech-style! *Brambore!* I used to think the name came from *brumbari,* the Colorado potato beetles that would infest our potato crops. Whenever that happened, terrible curses could be heard coming from the garden. *Fuck you and your Coloradan whore of a mother,* Grandpa would hiss through his teeth while running toward the cellar, where he was brewing up a hellish concoction for their Coloradan whore of a mother.

Our cuisine was influenced by the Czech tradition and cumin was always generously sprinkled on cabbage and potatoes.

The potato has a peculiar structure: smooth and hard when peeled, yet when given the right treatment, it can become quite fluffy. The secret of Czech potatoes is in the cutting, the amount of water, the temperature, and the shaking.

Czech Potatoes

Take a pound of potatoes, one and a quarter sticks of butter and a half-teaspoon of whole cumin seeds.

Cut each medium-sized potato into four or five large pieces. The water should reach to three-quarters the height of the potatoes. Add a little salt. Crank up the burner at first, let the mixture boil for about five minutes, then reduce it to the lowest heat. Cover with a lid. This steams the potatoes, opening their cells and making room for the butter. When the water has almost boiled off and there is less than half a centimeter left in the pot, it's time for the whole cumin seeds (or dill, if the potatoes are fresh). Where there's butter, there's always room for seasoning. And now comes the time for the shaking. Grasp the pot firmly by both handles and the lid and shake it, letting the shaking start from your ass and flow throughout your whole body like belly

3

dancing. The pot ends up on the periphery of the shaking, where the vibrations are more delicate, exactly right for steamed potatoes swimming in butter. Keep shaking and exhale downward toward the earth through your legs, because otherwise you just might fly off somewhere right along with the potatoes—and after such scents that just wouldn't be fair to the hungry inhabitants of the house. Return the pot to the heat for a few seconds to let it bubble up again and then repeat the shaking procedure several times, so that the fluffiest upper layer of potato collapses, laying bare new space for the butter to seep into. Czech steamed potatoes go well with salad, but are also a wonderful side dish for oven-baked cabbage, fish, or meat. Steamed potatoes are especially well suited to chicken livers with onion (Grandma's recipe again).

Chicken Liver with Onion

Take three medium-sized onions, a pound of chicken livers, four medium tomatoes, black pepper, butter, and two hot peppers.

Sauté the onions in butter along with the finely chopped hot peppers until they grow pink. Add the chicken livers, cut in half or smaller, then stir them with the onions for just a few minutes before adding the already-thickened sauce from the grated tomatoes. Follow by adding black pepper and salt, and let it all simmer together for three more minutes.

Grandma's potato secrets were inexhaustible. After exploring the sea and the dunes all day, there was nothing more lovely than catching sight of her grating potatoes. That meant *batz*, a type of Czech potato pancake.

Batz

Mix a cup of milk with four medium-sized grated raw potatoes, four cloves of garlic, parsley, two eggs, a dash of baking soda on the tip of the spoon, salt, and

flour. Keep adding flour until the mixture resembles
thin porridge.

Then Nikula would get out her big black frying pan and set it on
the fire. She'd add a splash of oil in the bottom and two ladlefuls of the
mixture. We would fall silent, our eyes fixed on the pancake and the deft
movements with which Grandma tossed it into the air. Batz!

We batzed ourselves silly until we flopped on the couches in a stupor,
listening to Radio Sofia. Whether it was folk or classical music, we completely trusted the taste of our one and only radio station.

Despite the fact that some nations completely despise the potato as a
boorish food, given my experience in mastering Czech potato traditions
(which are, in fact, German) I've continued to perfect the art of cooking
this tuber. Years later, I'm building again. My husband and I are restoring
an old village house in the southern Rhodope Mountains and I'm still
experimenting with potatoes from my very own garden. The first local
recipe I try is

Arse-End Potatoes

In the Rhodopes Arse-end potatoes are still cooked in the
traditional way, in an earthenware dish. It is crucial
to get your hands on such a pan, with low sides and a
thick bottom, glazed, if possible. Peel the potatoes and
cut them in half lengthwise, put a spoonful or two of oil
in the bottom of the pan, and arrange the half-potatoes
with the arse-end up. Sprinkle them with a thread of
oil, salt, and a little paprika for color. Bake them in
a preheated oven for around ten minutes until the tops
grow rosy, then place them over a low fire. This fries
the potatoes from below, bakes them on top and steams
them in the middle. A delicious reddish crust forms on
both sides, while the inside turns to purée.

Over the years, after planting my own rosemary, I've
elaborated on this recipe. I now grease the bottom of
the pan with olive oil and sprinkle it with crushed
rosemary needles. I cut the potatoes lengthwise, into
slices no more than 8 mm thick, and arrange them like
roof tiles. On top, I add another thread of olive oil,

5

crushed rosemary, and a pinch of hot red pepper to make
them smile. The baking principle is the same as with
arse-end potatoes. Afterward, it's like eating Bibles:
with your fingers, page by page—the scent of a shrine,
of holiness.

Granny Sweetest, Granny Dearest

At sundown, after yet another work-filled day, Grandma would sit down to read—usually *War and Peace* by Lev Nikolayevich Tolstoy. She would read through a big magnifying glass, quietly pronouncing each letter separately and then the whole word strung together one more time. Her red, cold-curled hair extended like antennae from the strain. As she read, she would become small, studious, and not the least bit terrifying, like in the poem by Dora Gabe:

> Mum said Granny was once a little girl,
> with long hair braided down her back,
> going off to school, notebook in hand.
> Good God, it's so funny to imagine
> my granny so old and gray,
> with a notebook, in a short dress,
> Granny sweetest, Granny dearest!

Nikula lost her mother when she was two years old, and her father remarried a wicked stepmother. Grandma was put to work at a young age, she had an amazing voice, and she was pretty—the only thing missing was the fairy godmother. My grandfather showed up instead and stole her away. He came from a family of gardeners, and like his father before him, he soon left to work in gardens in Hungary, Austria, and Germany. He would come back now and again, make another child and then go back to his tomatoes. My grandmother brought up her children alone with the money he sent her. She worked in strangers' fields and stored up intense rage toward him, since he wasn't around to witness her heroics. Her rage, hard-set with the years, would liquefy in the evenings, when the day was on its way out and she—in Czech or Bulgarian, depending on the holiday-maker's nationality—would complain about my grandfather for hours. In these stories, Grandpa Boris went by the name of "Sersemin"—in Turkish *sersemin* means "scatterbrained." The Sersemin this, the Sersemin that, while she was the long-suffering heroine. It made you wonder why she kept having his kids. For many long years, I have tried to shake off that whining.

Despite the fact that he no longer travelled abroad, Boris rarely put in an appearance during the years when Nikula looked after me because they always needed cash. The house was gluttonous, and on top of that I don't think he felt like hanging around at home with my grandmother. At one point, he worked in the mines in Madzharovo, since surely there was no longer much money in gardening. Sometimes my grandma and I would take the train and embark on the long journey to visit him. My grandfather was a cheerful person who looked like Jean Gabin. He had a flair for entertaining people, for telling endless stories from his travels, and when it came to belly dancing and playing the tambourine, no one could hold a candle to him. He would have whole wedding parties howling. My grandmother hated him most of all for that—for the fact that he had never stopped having fun, while she had stuffed her joy down a rabbit hole when she was still a child so that there would only be room left for *useful* things! I only rarely heard her sing. For her, dancing and craziness didn't have any use, so she treated them with scorn—or rather, with the envy of her punished soul. Although on the occasions when we did go wild, she would laugh along with us. She envied my grandfather for another thing as well: for his gift for making money from everything. Even during the winter, when he stayed home, he would weave baskets and jugs from willow boughs, so sturdy and beautiful that the housewives would fall all over themselves to buy them. In principle, the housewives were always falling all over themselves for him anyway because he made them laugh, flirted with them masterfully, and knew exactly what to say to each one of them—which especially aggravated my grandmother. Later, when he was too old for the mines, he donned a dark blue uniform with yellow epaulets for his job as doorman at the Hotel Burgas in Sunny Beach. His cheerful blue eyes and mischievous mastery of Hungarian, Czech, Russian, and German frenzied whole flocks of female fans. They filled his wallet with generous tips, and these windfalls trickled down to me, too.

Baked Rabbit

I liked my Uncle Klemo much better than my Aunt Maruna, who really annoyed me. Klemo took after Grandpa, he'd inherited his blue eyes and he and my mom were a team. When he and Maruna came back on weekends from the boarding school in Burgas, we'd go to the movies, not that there was any great selection. They always showed *Mr. Pitkin, Parts 1 and 2*. It was a comedy, and the only part I remember is the scene where Mr. Pitkin dresses up as a nurse and tries to walk in high heels. Dressed up in my mother's nursing coat and her size 41 clodhoppers, my uncle would imitate that scene so brilliantly. We'd roll on the ground, stomping our feet and peeing ourselves with laughter. Grandma, too. It was funnier than in the film.

At that time, Klemo and Maruna had just taken up smoking. When they came back home, they would sneak cigarettes amongst the cornflowers at the far end of the yard near my turtles. I kept their secret, but blackmailed them into buying me candied fruit. Once, Rufi and I found a kitten and secretly kept it up in the attic because Grandma didn't want us coddling any animals inside the house—she'd had enough with my grandpa's stupid wolfhounds. I showed the cat to my uncle, and he grew silent and angry. He told me to forget about the kitten and took it away to Burgas. There was no one I could complain to, but he made me so mad that I tattled on him to Grandma for smoking.

God, all hell broke loose the next time he came home. The whole house shook with their stomping and shouts. Grandma chased him with a dustpan; you could hear the dull ring of metal hitting bone. Klemo howled, while Nikula's voice pierced the din.

"You worthless brat, yesterday's turd. So you're smoking on me, are you? Just like that rapscallion, your father! I raised you from a mere slab of flesh," she screamed, laying into him. "Now you're gonna poison yourself. Once you're earning your own money, go ahead and buy shit for all I care, but don't you dare buy tobacco with my money!"

I listened to the uproar with satisfaction, since for once somebody besides me was getting a thrashing, but I soon felt sorry for my uncle and began to get scared. It was dangerous to unleash Nikula's fury. I had just breathed a sigh of relief that the attack seemed to be tapering off when the dustpan came down hard on my back.

"Whyyyyyy," I screamed as I writhed at her feet.

"So you learn not to tattle, you worthless brat!"

Thus my grandmother concluded our lesson for that evening and disappeared behind the curtain by the kitchen sink, where she rattled the dishes around for quite some time. After such campaigns, she would let off steam with cleaning.

After a week, I made up with my uncle. I apologized for ratting him out and he told me the following story. Once, in Czechoslovakia, after many unsuccessful attempts, he finally managed to sweet-talk Nikula into letting him adopt two small kittens. They named them Topsy and Mopsy, and they soon grew into magnificent cats, everybody's darlings, especially Nikula's. They adored her and would wallow in her lap for hours in the evening. For Christmas, the family slaughtered a pig, made sausages, and put them in the cellar to ripen. Somebody left the cellar door open, and Topsy and Mopsy snuck in, gobbled up whatever they could, chewed on the rest and then escaped.

Nikula discovered the damage but didn't say anything, which wasn't a good sign. Instead, she threw away the remains of the sausage and rattled around the kitchen, sunk in a deep silence. Topsy and Mopsy were nowhere to be seen. The next day, the whole family gathered for dinner. The delicious aromas of baked rabbit and apricot dumplings wafted from the kitchen.

This fragrant dinner lightened up the gloomy atmosphere of the preceding days. They ate and drank, and at one point Boris asked: "Well now, woman, where are Topsy and Mopsy?"

"How should I know? They ran away, like the devil's spawn they are. How could they dare come back now," my grandma replied angrily.

Boris pushed the food around on his plate and set down his fork. The children followed him closely with their eyes. All at once, the whole gang realized what had happened and rushed outside en masse to throw up in the yard. They went to bed hungry; the next day they had dumplings for breakfast and slunk away silently.

Grandma tossed out the pan of "rabbits," but a month later she appeared in a leather vest, lined with fur on the inside since, of course, cat-fur vests work wonders for a sore lower back.

"You know her favorite cat-fur vest? The one she never parts with," Klemo asked, finishing off his story.

How could I not know it? I had worn it myself.

"So now do you see why I let the kitten go?"

And Hollywood tries to give me their *Addams Family*. What a joke!

Potato Dumplings with Fruit

Boil the potatoes in the evening, and on the next day peel them and grate them using a fine grater. Add two eggs, flour, and a bit of semolina to make dough that won't stick to your hands. Form it into small balls wrapped around the pitted fruit. Bring salted water to a boil, then stretch cheesecloth across the pot and secure it with an elastic band. Place four to five dumplings on top of the cheesecloth and cover with a lid. Steam the dumplings for 20-25 minutes. Dissolve cinnamon and sugar in butter and pour the sauce over the finished dumplings, or add poppy seeds and sugar to the butter as desired.

Dumplings with Yeast

Take one packet of dry yeast, one cup of flour, one cup of semolina, one cup of milk, one egg, and one tablespoon sugar.

Mix the yeast, sugar, several spoonfuls of warm milk, and one to two spoonfuls of flour and set aside to allow the mixture to rise. Once it has risen, add the remaining flour and semolina. Stir the egg and a pinch of salt into the remaining milk and add it to the mixture. Knead the stiff dough and let it rise for an hour. Then, knead it again and shape it into a long loaf. Cut it into three or four pieces like small rolls. Wrap them in a clean towel and let them rise for twenty minutes. Drop them into boiling salted water and let them cook for five minutes covered with a lid. Then remove the lid, flip the dumplings over, and finish boiling them in an open pot for five more minutes. After removing them from the pot, pierce the boiled dumplings in several places and cut them into slices with a strong thread. Serve them with roasted meat, gravy, and oven-baked cabbage. As with the potato dumplings, you can wrap fruit in the dough and drizzle it with butter, sugar and cinnamon, or poppy seeds.

Gnomes and Gardens

My grandmother was a good gardener, but the garden that Grandpa created on the acre around the house was magical. Our house was built in the new part of Nesebar near a forest, amidst huge sand dunes. It was finally my grandma's own house and her own garden after so many years of trials and tribulations with six children in *fureign* houses in *fureign* lands. The garden thrived on the sand, and my grandfather worked his magic. Flowers and vegetables previously unknown in these parts appeared—and little clay gnomes! No one had even dreamed of garden gnomes back then. One was a hunter with a rifle and a rabbit in his hand; another gathered mushrooms in the basket on his back, which filled up when it rained. There was a lazy, mischievous, lounging one, as well as industrious gnomes with all sorts of tools thrown over their shoulders. Slightly shorter than me, they were my dolls; I fashioned clothes for them from flowers. I was convinced that mercury came from the droplets on the leaves of the watercress and velvet from the petals of the dahlia, and corn silk made fantastic coiffures.

In our garden, vegetable crops alternated with rows of flowers. Marigolds, tagetes, and nasturtiums separated the potatoes from the carrots and peppers. The herbs blanketed everything with fragrance: rosemary, celery, basil, dill, anise, coriander, lovage, mint, pennyroyal, marjoram, sage. At the very end of the garden, beyond the cucumbers and pumpkins, lived a family of turtles, whom I lulled to sleep in a cardboard box. Grandpa made the garden fence out of fresh poplar cuttings that took root. It didn't take long before our garden was ringed by a thick wall of saplings. Boris set colorful, decorative gourds to creep up their trunks, which rattled in the wind and scared off the birds. Amidst the fruit trees, there was also a scarecrow with red wavy hair, which resembled Nikula when she was enraged. Besides the usual sorts of tomatoes, my grandfather was very proud of his orange tomatoes and yellow peppers; meaty and massive, they were brought from Hungary, but the seedless oxheart tomato with its delicate pinkish hues was still the most delicious.

For the first seven years of my life, I didn't even know what a green-grocer was, or a telephone or television. Whenever we needed something, I was told to go and get some cabbage near the fence or some potatoes next to the nasturtiums. Somewhere around that time, I learned to eat hot peppers. When Grandpa sent me into the garden to pick some of his pep-pers for him, he told me to pluck one of the baby ones for myself, which were slightly spicy. I was the fussiest eater in the world. My grandma got it into her head that the only way to save me was for me to start eating spicy foods.

I was scrawny, baked by the sun, with long, dark hair down to my shoulders. I look like an Indian in photos from that period. I would wear white, sagging pants, and woolen socks, sewn by my grandma to the soles of old sneakers cut to fit my foot. These were pretty uncomfortable, be-cause in the toe something like a sand bomb would form, with its own, independent trajectory. I had two dresses and one pair of shoes, which were saved for more dignified occasions. Most of the time, I tramped around barefoot.

It was poverty with a capital P. Aunt Maruna, after coming home and carefully putting away her school dress, would pull on some reworked skirt of Grandma's, with no panties on underneath. Who'd buy you those extras? The dresses in the attic were not to be touched. When I wanted to get back at Maruna for something, I would wriggle under her skirt and lift it high over my head in front of the other kids or the workmen in the yard. Maruna would scream and chase me, until Grandma caught us and lifted us both up by the ears.

I didn't have any toys, but as compensation, besides the gnomes, all the construction tools were at my disposal: pliers, an adz, a hammer, nails, lumber. With them, I crafted various contraptions. These undertakings led to my interest in building and to the creation of dozens of little houses, huts, and other dwellings. This proved to be an unenviable passion, since I seemed to be the only one gripped by it. Immediately after our initial rush of excitement to make a fort, the other kids' enthusiasm would evaporate and I usually had to finish building it on my own. Afterward, however, I could never drag them out of what I'd just cobbled together from scraps of rugs. In the evening, they'd show up with potatoes and peppers, asking, "Why don't we light a campfire? Why don't we roast these and all live together in the little hut?"

Leftovers

I'm certain that Grandma hated Grandpa so much because he was always gone. Nikula had a family, but it consisted only of herself, her children, and the wedding photo on the wall, from which she and my grandfather gazed out determinedly. How delicate her chin was in that picture. According to the fashion of the time, both of them wore straight Astrakhan hats, which gave their high-cheekboned faces an Asiatic fierceness. On Boris, she dumped the blame for her hard lot and for all the evils in the world.

Whenever he would come back, after a brief spell of joy, Grandpa would struggle to recognize the idea of this family that he had carried with him here and there, while she would feel quite awkward with her actual husband, whom she would have liked to love. Yet the Sersemin, at whom she had so many accusations to hurl and whom she had cursed so many times in her loneliness, cast a heavy shadow, and soon they both sank into silence. So Nikula's love most often took on the form of various smaller and larger acts of spite. God, the kinds of things she concocted for him to eat, despite the fact that she was usually an excellent cook. Often, she would crumble up the leftovers from a few days earlier into an aluminum dish. He would wonder what on earth it could be, while she quietly hemmed something or crocheted colorful little roses from which she later would make pillows and bedspreads.

When Grandpa would begin his dinner, Grandma would never sit down at the table with him. She would take bites as she cooked, and was always nibbling on something standing up or wiping some pan with bread crust. She claimed that she had a delicate stomach and that she couldn't eat our food. Grandpa would push what passed for food around his plate. Nikula would watch him slyly over her glasses, waiting for him to explode. But he wouldn't let on. For the time being, he would play the game. The clock in the kitchen would kill off the minutes one by one. At a certain point, however, he couldn't take it anymore and would burst out: "Manda, girl, go get me some of those hot red peppers near the gourds. And one,

15

no two, two heads of garlic."

When I returned, he would crush the garlic under his strong palm, I would peel a whole heap of the cloves and he would dip first the peppers, then the garlic, into the salt and scoop up a little of his dinner. He would top it all off with thick slices of bread. His eyes would water, turning from blue to green. Sweat would roll down his forehead and fire would come from his mouth. Grandpa would sniffle and snort. Worked up by the hot peppers, he would hum a Romanian tune, belch loudly, and drag out the homemade brandy to put out the fire. At that point, Grandma would carefully set aside her knitting and go out to stroll through the fresh air in the garden, completely helpless before the fact that his presence was more unbearable than his absence.

Of course, there were other dinners, as well. At the sight of the same crap, he would suddenly get sick of playing at "I eat your absence, and now you eat slop" and would push aside the plate, saying somehow kindly, wearily: "Come on now, woman, what are these leftovers you're giving me again?"

Grandma, crushed by this intonation, would stare at the food as if seeing it for the first time, digging around in it with a fork: "Well, it's food, and mighty tasty, too."

And Boris would head off for the mines in Madzharovo again.

Fried Chicken

After several months, Grandma would play the dutiful wife again, as was expected, and we would set off for Madzharovo. We would change trains; I would press my nose to the glass and let my eyes and the landscape stir up the journey. Behind me, the adults' conversation buzzed cozily and I would let it swoop out toward the little stations, mountains, and fields. Grandma had an astonishing ability to move others, making them feel for her. Her heroic life created other landscapes behind me, crisscrossed by clucking tongues and exclamations. Traveling combined with drama brings on sharp attacks of hunger; the people in the compartment would exchange glances and pull out their greasy newspapers full of goodies. Oh, train food! There is nothing more delicious than the requisite fried chicken and hard-boiled eggs.

I didn't eat eggs then. It was only years later that I began eating them out of love in the form of eggs *à la arménien*. My future husband, an Armenian, made them for me one morning. Back then, he still brought me breakfast in bed. Once he returned with a tray, enveloped in the scent of toast and coffee, and triumphantly announced: "Eggs à la arménien!" How could I not try them?

Eggs à la arménien

Soft-boil five or six eggs very lightly—for no more than two minutes. During that time, put slices of black bread through the toaster twice, so that they become hard, and quickly cut them into little squares no larger than a half-inch. Put a stick of butter sliced into chunks on the warm bits of bread—the bowl should also be warmed. Salt the mixture and toss the peeled eggs on top. Stir carefully until the bread is lacquered with egg. This way, the sulfuric taste of the boiled egg is hidden behind the scent of the butter and the toasted

17

black bread. If the eggs are fresh from the farm, all the
better. Little lacquered squares. Orange ones!

Serve with a cup of hot coffee after making love in bed.
Follow with cuddling and deep sleep.

And for after that deep sleep, I know an unbeatable sandwich. I discovered it by accident, thanks to my current love.

Sandwich for 11 a.m. Hunger Pangs

Mash up half a handful of blue cheese with the same
amount of cottage cheese. Spread the mixture on a toasted
slice of black bread and top with large chunks of baked
eggplant, seasoned only with salt and olive oil. A glass
of red wine will open it up.

But getting back to the train, where the culinary rapture is in full swing. Besides the fried chicken and boiled eggs, my grandma pulls out a tomato as large as a child's head, one of the pinkish oxhearts. Compliments about her gardening prowess fly. A bottle of wine appears. For me, they cut it with lemonade in a thick plastic cup. We gobble down the food. They exchange recipes and addresses. Leaving the compartment, it is hard to part with people who have already become members of our family.

When I turn 33, I become friends with Buba, a Bulgarian woman who for years has been married to a rich Jew from Paris. They live in a house across from the Bois de Boulogne. One day, she tells me, he gives her a Porsche and they decide to try it out on a trip to Bulgaria. They've only been driving for an hour or so when Buba pulls out a basket from behind the seat and starts peeling boiled eggs and unwrapping fried chicken bundled in newspaper.

"What's that," Andre asks.

"The road makes you hungry, we need a little snack," Buba replies.

"But won't we stop to eat somewhere," Andre whines.

"We'll stop," Buba replies. "I made this for along the way."

Just try to explain these travel rituals to Andre in the Porsche! I'm sure that Buba had herself a nice little snack without batting an eye, maybe she even mischievously patted her insolent red curls with greasy little

18

fingers. Every autumn, Buba takes a plane from Charles de Gaulle and lands in Sofia, so as not to miss the redolence of *rooaasted reeed peeeeppers*. She likes stretching out her vowels like that. She especially likes spicing them up, too. I've never heard talk as *taaaasty* as hers anywhere. It's been days since we left her Paris home of stories, crackers, and coffee. There's no sleep. But Buba is another book.

Cherry Stain

At the far end of the yard, next to the brick wall of the neighboring house, there is a ripe cherry tree. It grows on the border of our gardens, so each family picks it from their side.

Today I'm wearing a dress, a white one, from my grandma Vera in Sofia. Stretched out on a thick branch, Rufi is eating cherries, spitting the pits at the cat and pretending not to see me.

"All black cats should be destroyed. Especially this one, 'cause it eats our cherries," he says.

"Gimme one."

"Did you see that? It went straight into its ear."

"Gimme a cherry."

"Here."

"That's not a cherry."

"It's a little pear. Check it out, it's silver."

"It's just a regular old light bulb for a lamp."

"This is no regular light bulb. If I drop it, it'll explode, and the whole world will die."

"You're lying!"

"Should I drop it?"

"C'mon, don't."

With the light bulb in his mouth, Rufi slowly climbs down out of the tree.

"It's just a lie, right? So why don't I just give it a whack and we'll see whether everyone dies?"

"Everyone who?"

"Your grandpa, your grandma, everybody."

"And me?"

"And you."

Silence.

He wiggles a brick out of the wall. I'm watching the light bulb from the ground.

"The world's not inside," I venture.

"No? Then how does it get inside the television?"

"Will you die, too?"

"I'll be the only one left."

"Why?"

"Why? Because I was the first one to find it!"

Silence.

"You're a jerk."

"OK, fine then."

Rufi raises the brick as if to strike. I kick him. We go rolling onto the ground. He shoves me toward the wall, grabs the brick and holds it over the light bulb again.

Above us, the cat, its paw hanging in midair, wonders why these two creatures aren't moving anymore. The wind tugs at my dress. In the silence, only the sound of overripe cherries hitting the ground can be heard.

"I'm letting it go now."

Silence.

"It's your own fault," he taunts.

"Don't, please."

"There's no use in begging."

"C'mon, please."

"OK, OK, since you're that upset, I won't. Buuuuut in that case."

"But what?"

"You have to take off your panties."

Silence.

"No."

"Look, I just have to move this little finger and the brick falls."

"No, no!"

"I won't tell anybody."

"No, I don't want to."

He slowly lifts the brick. I hurl myself on top of him. There's a crunch and a scream.

We lie there clutching at each other. I can't tell whether we're both dead or whether we're alive and if we're alive, whether the others are dead. An ant crawls over Rufi's leg. The cat carefully jumps down. Someone has scribbled across the sky with chalk.

"Mandaaa, Mandaaa. Where are you, girl," Nikula's voice comes calling.

"Mandaaa. I'mgonnatearoutyourhair."

"Grandma," I'm running and bawling.

"Wait a second," Rufi shouts after me.

"No!"

"Please, Manda, at least let me kiss you."

"No way."

"On the cheek?"

"Grandma won't stand for it. I'll tell her everything."

"See if I care, you little shit. Just you tell her. I'll burn down your whole house. I'll kill your garden gnomes. I'll shoot your dogs."

I slam the garden gate and bolt it.

"God almighty, just take a look at yourself. Why are you bawling?" Nikula looms above me, frightening and solid.

Silence.

"Blood! What's this blood here?" She points at a large stain on my dress.

"Grandma. I, I saved the world from dying."

"Go on inside and take it off so I can wash it. That'll teach me not to put a dress on you again."

Dolphins and Lemon Cream

During the winter and in the early spring, when it was neither construction nor gardening season, my grandmother busied herself with my education. She put together a serious program of study, consisting of learning Czech from children's books and practicing household skills, which, in her opinion, every girl ought to master. In the morning, I had two hours of Czech, with sewing lessons as a break. How to thread a needle, how to tie a knot, how to sew on a button, how to mend a sock, crocheting, backstitching, tacking, and hemming. The quick and dexterous washing of dishes was also a sort of wizardry unto itself—preparing the water, soaping, rinsing. Sweeping and washing the floor. Peeling potatoes, onions, and garlic. Cooking. Folding clothes. In spring I took part in hoeing the garden, weeding, planting the sprouts, reinforcing the greenhouses, painting, and spraying the fruit trees. As I made progress with my Czech and with my household and gardening skills, my grandmother's gaze softened. She coddled me with pancakes and unlocked the cupboard with minty *Lukche* hard candies and *Mu* caramels. On these days, peace, coziness, and order ruled the house.

In the afternoon I was free to do as I pleased. In the evening, before going to bed, Nikula would stand in front of the mirror and put thick layers of lemon cream on her face. She didn't have a single wrinkle. When she wasn't reading Tolstoy, she would tell me fairy tales—she only knew two—about the fox who played dead and tossed the fish out of the cart, and the story about the goat who sang: *Butchered, butchered, but not quite dead!*

Grandma always slept on her back, stretched out like a board. She was warm, and her whole being exuded the scent of lemon. Surely somewhere in the labyrinths of her life that sweet morning sleep had left her, because at 4:30 every morning, Nikula was up and at it, ready for heroics. For starters, that meant running barefoot on the beach. All the energies are awake at that time and the sea gives off iodine fumes, or so she said. In early spring we slept out on the porch, to toughen up. Its walls were made of climbing plants that blossomed with tiny white flowers, but they couldn't stop the sand, which flew in off the big dunes around the house. In the mornings when I awoke to the seagulls' cries, sand crunched in my mouth. Before I knew what was happening, I was already following my grandmother down to the beach with chattering teeth, her sweater tossed over my shoulders. At that time of day, the surf was as gentle as a kitten. Even the sea felt like sleeping that early. From those jogs I clearly remember only the cold, her exquisite, tanned legs peeking out from beneath her gingham skirt, and the dead dolphins tossed up on the shore.

Now every morning I look at my legs, which are the same as hers, and wonder what to do with that furious urge to run and work from the early hours. But then I remember that I used to love sleeping in.

In the period of my early morning sprints with Nikula, the local fishermen often illegally bombed the fish with dynamite to kill more of them at once. The fish would float to the surface, torn apart or stunned, and ready to be gathered up. Such blasts would sometimes take out dolphins as well. There were a few spots where the beach cleaners would pile up the dead dolphins, and Rufi and I, plugging our noses, would go to watch them rotting away. Their skins mummified and lasted longest, black and hard, while the contents turned to white worms that eventually dried out, too.

A fish bomb killed Rufi's father, and it was then that I saw a dead man for the first time. Since only the upper part of his body remained, in the coffin there was a soccer ball where his legs had been. Rufi claimed that his father was only pretending to be asleep, while I didn't dare to breathe because of the room's sweetish smell. I dashed outside and threw up.

After that, I stopped visiting the dolphin graveyard and forgot about death.

Blood

We often went to play on the swings at the elementary school. Once, after a rainstorm, a huge puddle formed beneath them. I suggested we line up some paving stones and lay some plastic on top so we could stop the swings without getting wet. The paving stones were soon lined up and covered with plastic.

Rufi jumped on and started swinging hard.

I yelled to him, "Wait for me to fix the plastic."

It was fluttering around and getting caught on the swing, but all that work had driven him into a frenzy and he didn't hear me, so I waited for the swing to go up high so I could fix our installation as much as possible. I managed it twice. There was only one corner left to tuck under the stones. I waited for Rufi to swing up high and . . .

When I came to, I was lying near the puddle, with the taste of iron in my mouth and an intense pain where my head should have been. I tried to get up, but I couldn't move. I wondered how my body could disobey me. There was no one in the schoolyard, but I remembered that I'd been with Rufi. I shifted and looked around—there, where I was lying, was a dark red stain in the dirt.

Somehow, I managed to reach the school's outdoor bathrooms. While I was trying to wash the blood from my hands and face, my legs gave out again. I made it to the sidewalk in front of the school and sat down, slumped against the fence. I was cold and shaking all over. I couldn't walk; I didn't know what to do. It was then that I understood for the first time that I am alone in my pain. It set me apart and there was no mistaking where I ended and where the world began. When I'm happy, I have no limits, but my pain is mine alone. Mine. I sat there and, as happens at such moments, I felt colors more intensely—it was sunset and the sea was mixing pink, purple, blue, and green. The sea in spring is very gentle. I wondered what to tell my grandmother. Would she beat me? I don't know how long I sat there, but somebody was saying something, nudging my shoulder. A strange woman.

"What happened?" she asked.

I told her it was from the swing.

"Let's get up now. What's your name?"

"Manda."

"Can you walk, Manda? We're going to the doctor."

"OK."

The woman grasped my arm firmly and we set off toward the old town. We were walking along the isthmus; this time it seemed endless to me. At some point, another woman stopped us.

"What's going on? Where are you taking that little Gypsy," she asked.

"To the clinic. I found her at the school."

I listened to this conversation as if from a distance, not even making an effort to raise my head. I looked myself over. I was wearing homemade checkered woolen slippers with no laces, thick homespun mud-spattered pants made from Grandpa's old trousers, and one of Maruna's T-shirts, now red. My long hair was matted with blood. I realized that I was poor. And badly dressed. I felt terribly ashamed—almost as much as the year before, when those of us from the lower grades went to greet the older kids at the start of the school year with poems. I had worked on my little verse all week with Nikula, but when my turn came, I went out onto the steps and began, "Oh, you bear, big bear . . ." At that moment I saw all those eyes fixed on me, I saw my mother's and grandmother's faces filled with expectation, and I forgot the poem. It seemed like I was standing there on those steps for ages. The kids started to laugh. I gathered my strength, took a deep breath and tried to think of some kind of ending: "Oh, you bear, big bear, how long your tail is." The audience burst into such unrestrained laughter that I ran back toward the teacher. I wanted to be invisible.

Now, the same as then, I wanted to be invisible as I stood there with those unfamiliar women. My legs started shaking even harder.

The women were chattering away. I heard myself say: "I'm not a Gypsy. I'm Manda."

They suddenly seemed to remember me and we hurried toward the clinic. There, the doctors shaved my head around the cut, stitched up my scalp and even put in a few staples so the wound wouldn't open up. They bound up my whole noggin, and one nurse who lived near us led me home.

They told me to lie down and not get out of bed for three days. Nikula freaked. She put me to bed and made me soup. She was silent, scurrying back and forth, clearly angry. I felt guilty. The silence weighed on me. If only she would yell a little bit!

In the evening my mother came back from the sanatorium and when she saw me all bandaged up she almost fainted in the doorway. She rushed over to hug me, but grandma pulled her away: "That's enough of your mollycoddling. She'll get over it soon enough, just like a cat."

My mother hugged me and caressed me. Naturally, I felt like the hero of the evening, to whom nothing could be denied. Suffering has its advantages. Later I would sometimes bandage up my hand or foot and go to school like that, reaping the benefits.

I was mad at Rufi for a few days, but I forgot about his treacherous flight when he gave me a fantastic pair of pliers left by his late father, and once again we were friends.

Tomatoes

I used to love going to the monastery on the shores of the sea. Its whiteness thumbed its nose at the blue, it burned eyes at noon, while in the evening the shadows of the cypresses crept over it. The old folks said that the monastery was a gift from a rich man. Once, when a terrible storm overtook his ship, he promised St. Nicholas, the patron saint of sailors, that if St. Nicholas saved him, he would build a white stone church on the cape. St. Nicholas saved him, and since the stone in that region was gray, the man imported carved white stone all the way from Greece. The monastery and church of St. Nicholas gleamed white in the distance, filling the sailors passing by the cape with hope, since all the winds and currents really did meet there.

In the sheltered flagstone-paved inner courtyard there was a long wooden table around which the nuns gathered in the summer and early autumn to do their canning for the winter. "Tomato time," that's what they called it, and they were happy when I used to come with my grandfather to help them with the grape harvest, or with the apples, pears, and plums in the garden.

The abbess, Mother Efrosinia, was a sprightly woman. She would read the Bible to me and explain the parts I didn't understand. Sometimes we played hide-and-seek. She sang well in church and had a low, strong voice. She loved standing at the edge of the cliffs, looming over the sea, and although she was physically there, in fact she was elsewhere. In her habit, she looked like a tree struck by lightning; she wore her towering velvet hat, or *kamilavka,* tied with a black veil. She had a calm and cheerful soul. Her eyes had turned bluish-green from staring at the sea, but when she was angry, she glared dark green, and it was best to make yourself scarce.

Besides the five older nuns, there was also one new, young novice with a round white face. She was serious and somehow seemed affronted. She looked down, kept silent, and was always reading. I didn't like her and felt uncomfortable in her presence. A stern and merciless God watched me through her olive eyes and knew all of my past and future misdeeds.

Ever since he had donned his doorman's uniform with its epaulets, Grandpa had also been looking after the monastery garden. The ox-heart was ripening. This year the tomatoes were growing by the cartload and they could barely manage to pick them all. The nuns crossed themselves and thanked the Almighty. The monastery was famous for its tomato soup.

Tomato Soup

In one quart of salted water, thoroughly boil a finely chopped head of celery, three carrots, one pepper, three onions, and two green onions. Strain out the vegetables. In this broth, bring the juice of five grated tomatoes to a boil, along with two nests of vermicelli, a sugar cube (to soften the tomatoes' tart taste), a small cone of incense crushed into powder, and whole basil leaves. Can be served with grated cheese.

Whole cauldrons simmered, especially on holidays, no matter what the season. If it wasn't fasting time, the nuns would add cheese to the soup. On the table stood small pots of hot pepper paste, which Sister Evdokia concocted all by herself.

Evdokia's Hot Sauce

Boil a pound of finely chopped, extremely hot peppers in two cups of water. Mash through a sieve. Add the following to the resulting purée: a half-cup of brandy, three spoonfuls of sugar, the juice of one lemon, salt, and, if needed, another cup of water. The sauce can be seasoned with finely chopped basil or ground cumin, as desired.

People from the nearby villages who came for the holiday would eat soup, cry from the hot sauce, and put out the fire with the convent bread's thick crust and cold water from the spring—and sometimes with wine, too, if Mother Superior allowed it. The red soup made everyone loquacious and cheerful.

One day, at the start of tomato time, Grandpa and I set off around noon in the dog buggy. We had two giant wolfhounds that he hitched up to a cart just big enough for two people and a little luggage. The people in Nesebar had gotten used to my grandfather's eccentricities, but that dog buggy made him famous throughout the whole region. Boris had thought up this mode of transportation when he took over a pigsty in the village of Vlas, using the buggy to cart over the swill. Otherwise, he usually scooted around on his bike. The pigsty as an enterprise had come about when my mother's younger sister, Sara, wanted to study agriculture and had to have experience with farm work in order to apply. Grandpa installed some yahoo named Boncho with the pigs as a watchman, and he and Sara started up the pigsty in Vlas. Boris went around to the restaurants in Sunny Beach in his dog buggy, collecting slop in pails. Boncho kept watch over the pigs and got tanked, and, whenever he got hungry, helped himself to the least mangy meatballs from the slop. From time to time, Grandpa also found some horse on its last legs so the pigs could have fresh meat. Once, they brought over a blind, unfortunate horse. The pigs were hungry. Boncho was dead drunk. What else could Sara do? She tossed a sack over its head and whacked it with the butt of an ax (while looking the other way, of course). Afterward, once she had made sure it wasn't moving, she chopped it up. The pigs went crazy for it.

My aunt completed her internship, but never did end up studying agriculture, because right when she was supposed to apply, she fell in love with a handsome German choral director and, to my grandmother's great relief, got married and moved to Germany. More to the point, this was a great relief because Sara was a beauty and had my grandmother's wild nature. Hordes of admirers were always traipsing after her, and that "threatened the family's good name." My aunt's marriage in Germany was a particular source of pride for Nikula, something like an emblem of the family's success. Every summer, Sara would come and visit us with suitcases full of presents and her experiences abroad, with which she strengthened her belonging to the family.

It was fun traveling by dog, to say nothing of how proud I was to sit next to Boris in that strange vehicle. That day, when we reached the monastery, Mother Efrosinia had just finished parceling out the tasks. Grandpa disappeared somewhere into the garden. Around the big table under the vine-covered trellis, the nuns were working silently, as if speaking would make the tomatoes go sour. They were making tomato juice; peeled, canned tomatoes cut into large chunks; and thick tomato sauce with celery, parsley, and chili peppers in taller jars. They lugged over tubs of tomatoes; a huge cauldron of water was boiling on the fire so they could steam them for a few minutes right in the tubs to make the skins come off easily. After that, they peeled the tomatoes, cut them into large chunks, and stuffed them into the jars. Granny Petrania sealed the lids with a little machine. Her moustache was longer than Grandpa's.

Afterward, the full jars were arranged in a big black kettle, where they would be boiled for ten minutes. They gave me a sharp little knife so I could peel tomatoes, too. The young novice usually did the same job, but that time there was something wrong with both her wrists and they were bandaged up. She sat at the end of the table, clutching a small Bible, and from time to time would stop perfectly still, her gaze empty.

I adored holding a warm, stretched-to-bursting tomato in my hand. I had my own system for peeling them. First, I made a little cross on the backside and from there pulled each corner of red skin toward the green navel. After that I would cut the naked tomato into quarters and toss it into a big wooden trough. I was important. I was working right alongside the grownups. Sometimes, it seemed like I could hear the red juice pulsing in our veins. The wind, gentle and round there in the monastery's inner courtyard, rustled in the trellis. Its shadows played on our faces. From time to time, I noisily slurped up the thin streams of juice that trickled all the way down to my elbows, or ate the tomatoes whole when little ones came my way.

At the other end of the table, Evdokia stuffed the peeled tomatoes through a meat grinder for juicing. Her strong white fingers pressed them into the machine's insatiable throat, and I kept thinking that any minute her flesh would come out of the little holes, but she always managed to save her fingers and even licked them from time to time, eyes closed. Evdokia was the liveliest and cleverest of the nuns in the monastery. Her husband had been lost at sea during a storm, and her sons had run off to America. The authorities had dragged her in for interrogation after interrogation, and in the end finally left her alone. Then, to everyone's astonishment, she joined the monastery. She was pretty, with warm white skin and light-brown, almost yellow eyes. Instead of black, she wore a tidy dark blue habit that reached below her knees, and when she worked in the garden or at the big table, she put on a green apron with big orange flowers. Unruly copper curls often tumbled out from beneath her dark blue veil. I greatly envied her for that hair and dreamed that when I grew up, I would dye mine that color, too.

Petrania handed me a longish little tomato, and in my greediness I bit into it so ferociously that the seeds shot out and sprayed Mother Superior. Efrosinia blinked through the goo, covered in yellow seeds. I started to laugh, but the young nun shot me an angry glance.

"Ooh, Mother, it was an accident, I swear," I started apologizing, diving under the table to clean her up.

"Don't bother, my child, I was going to wash this habit anyway."

Then I noticed that right in the middle of her velvet *kamilavka,* the seeds had formed a perfect little cross.

"Mother, look. You've got a tomato cross."

"Holy Mary, Mother of God!"

The nuns crossed themselves. Mother Superior raised her eyebrows knowingly and smiled. Evdokia dumped yet another overflowing tub of tomatoes on the table.

"Mother, why do we cross ourselves?" I asked. "Didn't they crucify Christ on the cross? So that means the cross is something bad."

Mother Superior looked at me carefully and started to say something, but the young nun's voice cut in: "The cross is a symbol of the soul, crucified by the human body. The soul strains upward, but the body drags it back down to earth."

"But why did people kill God?"

"He is the Son of God," the young nun replied. "He was sent especially to earth so that through His sacrificial death man would be redeemed from his sins."

"So how can one person dying forgive everybody's sins?"

"Didn't I just tell you that He's not just one person, but the Son of God, who loved us so much that He sacrificed Himself for us and thus washed away our sins?"

"People are still bad today. He sacrificed Himself for nothing."

"You don't know how much worse things would be if He hadn't sacrificed Himself. The power of His love is great," she snapped.

"So does everybody who loves have to sacrifice themselves? If He loved us, why did He let them crucify Him? Couldn't He just have lived with us and loved us, instead of dying?" I insisted.

"He couldn't, because people are constantly tempted by the devil and they always commit sins. With His sacrifice, the Son of God weakened the power of evil. We are not worthy of Him."

"How did He weaken evil?"

"Oooof, Manda, you're too little to understand," the young nun shouted in an unexpectedly loud voice.

Mother Superior shot her a dark-green glance. I took this as reinforcement and pressed on. "So since Christ suffered, are only those who suffer good?"

"No, good people are all those who . . . ," Petrania started to explain.

"In that case, Grandma's good, because she's always suffering, while Grandpa is bad, because he's always out having fun."

"Your grandfather is tempted by the devil," hissed the young nun breathlessly, looking Evdokia straight in the eye. Flustered, the latter lowered her gaze.

". . . believe in the true faith," Petrania concluded.

The nuns waited to see how this unequal theological debate would end. Mother Superior continued filling the jars. In the intervening pause, I finished off my volley. "Grandpa isn't bad. He doesn't beat me."

"Look, my child," Mother Superior began in her deep voice, "a person wants to be good, but he is not bound to good alone. He can choose both to sin and to suffer. Choice is what separates us from the animals and brings us closer to God."

The table under the vines fell silent. I got the feeling that I was getting into something I didn't understand. I felt the truth somewhere within myself, but I couldn't express it. I started itching all over. I felt confined and I wanted to jump or run, so I told Mother Superior I was going down for a swim. Efrosinia nodded.

As soon as I poked my nose out of the monastery, the wind struck me. I closed my eyes and gave myself over to it. I blew through the branches of the almond trees, floated above the water, I was the soft grass on the hills, and at that moment, I knew.

I took off, running down the steep path to the sea. I dived in, dress and all, so as to wash the red juice out of it, then flopped down naked on the hot sand. Good thing it was a dark blue print with little violet roses, so the red didn't show much. I wore it when I went to the monastery, because once the young nun had said that it wasn't proper to tramp around the cloister in my underpants, as was my wont. I went back into the water. I really loved diving at the cape. Marble columns from some old temple gleamed on the sea floor, and there were huge, completely preserved jars in which all sorts of creatures hid. When I pounded on one of the jars, a silver wine of thousands of tiny fish frothed from the inside. I had just taken a breath to dive back down to the jars when from up above I heard my grandfather's piercing whistle. Only he could whistle like that; I envied him terribly for this. I was also a good whistler myself, so much so that when I got lost, which happened all too often, my grandpa could find me by my whistle. I swam toward the shore and, wet as I was, pulled on my dress, ironed out by the sun and the salt, and climbed up the steep path to the monastery.

Up above, Grandpa was lining up gifts on top of his old quilted jacket in the wooden cart—a bottle of amber plum brandy, a jar of hot chilies with tomato sauce, a basket of yellow pears, and ears of corn. Evdokia came running over carrying a loaf of bread with a little cross baked on top, waved goodbye to us, and we started bumping along the narrow dusty road through the almond forests—which made eating the corn really difficult.

At home, Nikula took one look at the gifts and knew we'd been to see the witches again, as she called the nuns. She tossed aluminum plates filled with leftovers on the table and sat silently somewhere on her beloved porch. Grandpa winked at me, and I went to pick some of the hottest chilies for him and some of their babies for me. When I got back with the peppers, he had already cracked open a big head of garlic.

Money

Rufi and I liked roaming the beaches most of all. We would lounge on the dunes, spy on the nudists, and swim in the sea despite the bans. Once the season started, we would use a flour sieve to sift the sand around the changing rooms, since money and all sorts of valuables would fall out of the pockets of those changing. The other way of gathering funds was collecting empty bottles. We would return them to the store and they'd give us some money. We would split up the day's haul. Rufi, who was older and in first grade, knew a thing or two about money. Gathering all the coins in his palm, he'd say, "Take your pick." I, of course, would take the little gold coins while he, to my amazement, picked the silver ones. Afterward when we went to the store, he would buy himself a whole box of chocolate bars and maybe even a soda to boot, while all I'd get were a few candies. This was surely because the clerk was some aunt of his and that's why she gave him more stuff. Once, we dug up a man's watch and decided that Rufi should wear it, since he was in first grade, knew what time it was, and was a man. We didn't tell anyone about our treasures; we squirreled them away in our secret hiding place in the fort we had built in the crown of a huge tree in the forest that began in front of our houses.

Once, at dusk, we found two silver fifty-cent pieces in the sand by the changing rooms and we split them up, each taking one. It was too late to go to the hideaway. At home, as I was getting undressed for my bath, the coin fell out of the Indian leather pouch around my neck. Grandma grabbed it and asked me where I'd gotten it from.

"I found it."

"You're lying! You stole it. Who'd you take it from?" Nikula insisted.

"I didn't take it from anybody! I found it."

"Where?"

"On the street in front of Rufi's house." We had agreed not to tell anyone about the trick with the sieve.

"You didn't say anything? You didn't ask whose it was?"

"There was nobody around!"

"Oh, so you waited for the guy to leave."

"What guy?"

"What were you going to do with it?"

"I don't know. Buy candy or soda."

"Good God, I'm raising a little thief." Nikula hurled herself onto the couch, like she had fainted. She was staring at the ceiling, where the instructions for what to do with terrible children were written. "Now I'll teach you a lesson!" She disappeared into the room where the sewing machine was. Soon she returned, held a needle in front of my face and asked, "Which do you prefer to be jabbed with: a hot needle or a cold one?"

Picturing the white-hot iron, I pulled away and started squealing: "Cooooold!"

"Fine," Nikula said. Sitting on a chair, she pressed me between her knees, stuck my left hand under her armpit so I couldn't defend myself and began quickly jabbing my right one, shouting: "This'll teach you not to take other people's money and things that don't belong to you, you miserable little thief!"

"I woooon't," I screamed from the pain, trying to break away and hoping somebody would appear. But the house was empty. My grandmother wasn't fooling; she laid into me with the needle like nobody's business, egging herself on in the name of honesty all the while: "My children don't steal! Where did this filthy little Sofian fiend pop out of?"

When I was sufficiently perforated, she let me go and told me, as calm as could be, "Stop crying. I'll disinfect it with iodine."

At the thought of the burning iodine, I bolted out of the house and slipped into the woods across the way. I ran until I reached the tree with the fort. My hand was bleeding and stinging. It was starting to get cold. Good thing we had brought an old blanket to the fort. I spread out some newspapers and curled up under the blanket. I heard Nikula calling me until late into the night, but I didn't dare go home.

My grandmother had a very fluid concept of honesty. In late autumn, she would organize the kids on hand and we would glean. Whatever the pickers had overlooked in the orchards and vineyards was ours. Our bags filled up with all sorts of earthly goods, some of which did not seem "overlooked" at all—unless, of course, the pickers had decided to pass over whole fields. There was some sort of joyful thrill in our quick and quiet roving through the fields by the sea at dusk. The best was when grapes were the target of our picking. If they were fit to eat, we would set some aside and dump the rest in a large wooden trough. My grandma would wash my feet with soap and then let me stomp the grapes until every last one was squashed. This made a thick, sweet nectar, which we strained and drank to our heart's content, then poured the rest into large glass bottles for wine.

At dawn I awoke in the fort, cold and in pain. My hand had swelled enormously, covered in scabs. I set off toward the sea through the almond trees. I wanted to wash my wounds with salt water. When I reached the monastery, the sun was already rising.

"Manda, where are you headed so early?"

Mother Superior's voice startled me. She was sitting down, leaning against a dried tree.

"To swim in the sea."

"Isn't it cold still? Come here, come here for a minute."

I hid my hand behind my back and wondered whether to approach her.

"Come here," Efrosinia said, and spread open the skirts of her wide habit. "First come here and get warmed up." I went over, sat down by Mother Superior and let her embrace me. Tears burst from my eyes. I hadn't known I wanted to cry. My whole body started shaking. Mother Superior pressed me close and stroked my hair. Her habit and hands always smelled like incense and thyme. I gradually calmed down and fell asleep. I was awakened by the sun, which was now blazing.

"Let me see."

"See what?"

"Your hand."

As she pulled it out from under her habit, two deep vertical wrinkles furrowed her forehead.

"Who did this to you?"

Silence.

"Come with me."

I pulled away. "Please, no iodiiiine."

"I'm not going to put iodine on it."

"Will it hurt?"

"It won't hurt—now come on!"

Mother Superior poured a mixture into a pan and washed the wounds with gauze dipped in the mix. It only stung slightly. Then she picked some stonecrop from the garden, peeled off the thin membrane, put it on my hand, wrapped it up in cheesecloth, and said, "Don't get it wet today. You can tell me when you're ready."

"Grandma. Because she thought I had stolen fifty cents. But I found it and picked it up. But she didn't believe me and punished me. She asked me whether I wanted cold or hot. I chose cold. Then I ran away. I slept in the tree."

Mother Superior kept silent, her face taut, and pressed me to her.

"Next time you find something, show it to her. Now go home, they'll surely be out looking for you. Come back tomorrow and I'll put some more stonecrop on it. And don't get your hand wet today."

When I got home, Grandma wasn't there. Grandpa was just going out. "Where have you been? We've driven ourselves crazy looking for you! What's wrong with your hand?"

"Grandma jabbed it yesterday because she thought I had stolen some money. I slept in the woods. Mother Superior wrapped it up with herbs."

He sighed. "I called your mother. She'll be here soon. I'm going to the monastery."

Yellow Roses

I was lying in the cellar. That's where we lived when there were vacationers in the house. Through the ground-level window I could see my mother's feet when they were going to or returning from her job at the health clinic. Her beautiful feet, shod in light beige shoes, so low-cut that you could see the base of her toes, with little doodads on the side and low square heels, a thin strap and open backs. I had already fallen asleep when she burst into the half-darkened room.

I sank into her soft, rustling embrace. How nice she smelled. She was wearing her favorite olive green dress with huge yellow roses and a plunging neckline, fitted at the waist and flared out below her knees. I loved that dress so much that I had once cut out one of those yellow roses, but Mama's seamstress had cleverly sewed it back on and it didn't show at all. I took a beating for that, of course.

"My dearest, sweetest little girl," my mother whispered. "What has my crazy mother done to you? Does it hurt?"

I snuggled up to her. My whole body shook with sobs. I begged her not to leave me with Nikula, to take me with her. But she couldn't. She worked in Vlas at a clinic for people with bone diseases. She was pulling double shifts in order to pay the lawyers to fight for me.

My paternal grandfather, an influential Sofia attorney, had been suing my mother for years to take away her parental rights and bring me back to Sofia. In front of the judges, he made her out to be the worst woman in the world—with the help of false witnesses. That's what Nikula said.

"Who bandaged you up?"

"Mother Efrosinia."

My mother hugged me and started to cry. It got really warm there pressed to her chest. It was so sweet to be together again. At that moment I caught sight of my grandmother's feet, and seconds later she burst into the room. She took one look and set upon us, trying to pull us apart. She always did that when Mama cuddled me.

"That's enough, now! That's enough mollycoddling her!" Nikula pulled at us, but we clung together. "That's why she'll never amount to anything!"

Grandma stalked around the cellar. When her conscience pained her, she would go around straightening things up, and that gave her the courage to dig in her heels all the more.

"Mother, quit hurting her. You can't treat her like this. She's only a child!"

"This is my house and my discipline. I'm not going to look after thieves. She comes in here, drags home some money, I have no idea where from."

"Fifty cents. I found it."

"Silence!" Nikula swatted with her heavy hand. "Don't you give me that cheeky look from behind your mother's back. If you run away one more time, I'll strangle you with my own bare hands and I'll do the time for it, if I have to. Making me go around the streets hollering like a lunatic all night! The whole town knows our business!"

My mother shielded me with her arms. "Don't you dare touch her. I won't stand for that."

"Well, if you don't like it, you're both free to leave!"

"There's nowhere for us to go."

"If you'd put up with your husband, you'd have a home in Sofia."

"No. I'm not going to put up with it. I'm never going to put up with that again. You put up with it if you want."

"I do put up with it, as you can see. Which is the only reason you have a roof over your head."

"Which you are kicking us out of. I forbid you to torment her!"

"That's my way of disciplining her. You never should have had her, since you don't have time for her."

"She would never have been born if you hadn't forced me to get married. My life would have been completely different."

At that point, they looked at each other and continued their row in Czech, as they usually did so I couldn't understand what they were talking about. But I had begun to understand that language better than they suspected. That's how I found out how my mother had come to marry my father.

"Nobody forced you into anything. You just sat there silent all night at the table when he came to ask for your hand."

"Have you forgotten that when it was almost morning," my mother hissed, "you said, 'Since you've been silent for so long, I'll take that as a yes.' And you told him, you told him that I accepted. I kept quiet. Nine months later this poor little wretch was born." My mother pointed at me.

The story of their marriage that I later heard from my father (always referred to in that house as "The Freak from Sofia") was that, as a veterinarian sent by the government to work on the seaside, he once went to the movies in the old town of Nesebar with a local colleague. When they took their seats, his friend waved to a pretty girl up in the balcony. My father turned around and was completely bowled over by my mother's beauty. At that moment he felt that she was *the* woman for him. He had never seen such beauty. She was green-eyed with short red hair, cut into a bob. He asked his friend to introduce him to her.

At that time, my mother was driving the local bachelors wild. She wore stylish flowered dresses and the European spirit of her Czech education. She had just finished nursing school, she rode horses, played accordion, drew, and sang. She dreamed of becoming an opera singer.

Luckily for me, she really was the most beautiful and intelligent of Grandma's daughters. She took after my grandfather in spirit; she had his eyes and smile, but got her slender figure from my grandmother. Red hot!

A week after he first saw her, my father turned up at the house and asked for her hand. Grandpa was surely gone yet again. The prospective suitor was a veterinarian from Sofia. Nikula was, in any case, at her wits' end trying to figure out how to safeguard her crazy daughters' charms. Having educated, honest, and prestigiously married girls—that was her idea of parental duty well-fulfilled. That was why my mother's return to Nesebar and the end of her marriage was seen by my grandmother as a shameful failure for the whole family.

"You're the wretch, since you can't even keep a family together," spat out my grandmother. "Your head is full of singing, having fun, just like that miserable Sersemin, your father. So you're gonna be an opera singer now, are you? Just shut your mouth and don't you give me any lip!"

My mother sobbed and hugged me, and we sank into her yellow roses together. Tears silently flowed from her eyes. I wiped them away and stroked her hair. I remember that I then wished with my whole heart to build a big beautiful house when I grew up, where the two of us could live and nobody would ever throw us out. As if reading my thoughts, my mother calmed down, snuggled up to me, and soon fell asleep. Nikula slammed the door and left, muttering, "Just wait till I get my hands on you when we're alone."

Rose Jam

Take five ounces of rose petals. Prepare a thin syrup from half a quart of water and two pounds of sugar, boiling it until it thickens slightly; add the rose petals and simmer for a bit. When the mixture thickens, add one teaspoon of citric acid mixed with a small amount of lukewarm water. After five minutes, remove the jam from the heat and pour into warmed jars.

Nettles

Otherwise, the summer rolled on freely and easily. Mama came home from her job less and less often. Maruna and Klement were on the school work brigades, picking peppers and tomatoes in the fields around Aitos. On his bike or in his dog buggy, Grandpa flew between the hotel, the pigsty, and the monastery, while Grandma finished up the interior of the house's top floor, which didn't stop her from renting out two rooms on the second floor and even the cellar. Czech girls smelling of suntan lotion and wearing high heels picked their way through the plaster, nails, and construction debris, and in the evening, when they didn't go out dancing at the restaurants, they'd listen to my grandma's life story, sitting under our fig tree with homemade brandy and fresh tomatoes, wearing concerned expressions and clucking their tongues in sympathy.

Once my grandma rented out our cellar room to two Czech girls, so we had to sleep under the porch where there wasn't even a window. Right from the very beginning, I didn't like them. They looked down on me and rattled on in their language, thinking I couldn't understand them. I heard one of them say that I was a dirty little Gypsy and that our house was totally disgusting. Another time one of them kicked over the little house I'd made for the hedgehog—the newest resident of my garden. She laughed as I scrambled to pick up the pieces. I swore to get revenge. I didn't care that she was so much older than me, the stupid cow.

Rufi and I often went swimming in the Devil's River, at the point where it ran into the sea. We'd catch little water snakes there and play with them; they were rubbery, dry, and fascinating. When we'd had enough of them, we would let them go back into the water. That day, while I was telling Rufi about the new Czech girls, all of a sudden a brilliant plan for revenge dawned on me. All day we gathered up water snakes and managed to fill up two jam jars. Rufi also insisted that we arm ourselves with another jarful of green grasshoppers, just in case. In the afternoon, while the Czechs were at the beach, we snuck into their room, opened up the jars and quickly slipped back out. Then we quietly began crafting a door for our wooden fort in the garden, waiting for the Czechs to return. We didn't want to miss the show. They eventually turned up in all their sweaty glory, stuffed into their skimpy beach dresses and clucking, "Ahoy, ahoy," then disappeared into the cool basement. For a few moments all was silent.

"Maybe they didn't come out of the jars or they died from their perfume," Rufi suggested.

Through screened window we could hear the splashing of the water in the bathroom and their cheerful chattering. Then out of the darkness of their room we heard the sound of creaking springs. They'd lain down on the bed, tired out from the beach. Even though Nikula had forbidden me from entering the guests' rooms, I'd frequently succumbed to the temptation of looking through their things.

"Their room is such a pigsty that they must've gotten lost," I guessed.

At that moment unearthly screams erupted. We were so startled that we dropped our tools and hurled ourselves at the window.

"Jeeeeeesus, Maaaaary and Jooooooseph!" they screamed, and threw everything they could get their hands on.

One of them was screaming bloody murder and hopping up and down. The whole room was writhing. The little snakes were swarming out of the shoes on the floor (years later, Spielberg would steal our idea in a similar scene with Indiana Jones and his girlfriend in the bowels of a pyramid). The Czechs tried to defend themselves with towels. The next second, however, they realized what a losing battle this was and came running out into the yard, tossing away their bras and panties as snakes and grasshoppers came flying out of them. They ended up out in the street stark naked.

It was a hilarious sight. The workmen had come out and were doubled over with laughter. Nikula, too—until she realized what was going on. It was just the time when everyone was coming back from the beach. The two Czech girls pointed at the house, pale-faced and naked, babbling incoherently. A crowd immediately gathered. Someone gave them beach towels to cover up with, and other concerned Czechs immediately rushed toward my grandmother. Everyone gradually got swept up into the story, which our tenants began to explain with bellowing and hand waving.

Nikula's face grew darker and darker. As she listened, her furious stare locked on me. I somehow began to realize what I had done, and that Nikula knew too. All of a sudden she became calm and businesslike, as only she could. She herded the frightened girls onto the porch, gave them drops of valerian and mint in sugar cubes, made them lie down, wrapped them up, and told them not to move. On her way out she locked them in, just in case. She chased away the crowd, bolted the gate from the inside, and quickly went down into the cellar with two of the workmen. We heard terrible curses coming from inside: "May your hands shrivel up!" was the tamest of them.

Afterward she came back out, walked over to us and said in a steady tone (which was the most frightening part of all): "You two get down there now and get all those creatures out of there. You're not coming out until it's done." Then she went to check on the girls.

Rufi and I cleaned the cellar of snakes and grasshoppers until it got dark, but they were still creeping around everywhere. We cleaned the whole next day, too. Then Nikula asked us if we were ready.

"No," we said to buy time. "We're gonna have to clean tomorrow, too."

"Tomorrow? What's this 'tomorrow'? Are you crazy? This house had better be rid of varmints by this evening! Period. That's the final deadline!" Nikula snapped.

The situation got worse and worse. During those two days, all the tourists had left the house.

It was no fun at all down in that cellar. By that point we had totally forgotten how it all had even started. We already regretted having collected so many critters and started to wonder what they liked to eat so we could lure out the ones still left.

"We could bring some dead rat and leave it here to rot and when they come out to eat it, we'll grab 'em," Rufi suggested. He was the king of stupid ideas.

"Yeah, right, and who's going to eat up the stench afterward?"

I sensed that nothing good awaited me. Nikula wasn't one to forget such things, especially the tourists' leaving. Rufi started to lose heart. He lay on the bed in despair, sighing. That was exactly what he did when he got sick of building forts and I had to finish them by myself.

By afternoon we'd found only one snake in one of the priss's shoes. They wanted to leave the house immediately after the incident, but Grandma had installed them up on the porch and enchanted them with her stories, cooked for them, brought them everything they needed, in the hopes that they'd forget about it by the time we'd cleaned the vermin out of their stuff. We brought everything out into the yard, shook it out piece by piece and put it into a basket hanging on the washbasin. The workmen hungrily eyed the lacy lingerie and whistled. Meanwhile, the Czech girls sat on the porch like wet chickens and watched the resuscitation of their belongings from afar. When we finished with their luggage, we went down into the cellar one last time. We turned everything inside out—there was no trace of any little creatures. At dusk, after Grandma had scrutinized everything in the basket and carefully packed it into their suitcases, the Czech girls finally left our house. On their way out, they glared at us furiously and let fly a string of curses. There was something about *prdel*—Czech for "ass." They told Nikula that they'd never set foot here again as long as they lived and that they'd warn everyone not to stay at Boris and Nikula's because their house was swarming with snakes and lizards.

"Snakes and grasshoppers," my grandma corrected them, and angrily slammed the gate in their faces. Then she sent Rufi home and told him to be ready for the inspection tomorrow.

The next day was a Sunday. There were no tourists or workmen around. Rufi came over—he didn't abandon me this time. We started the final inspection with Nikula. She walked ahead, while we trailed at her heels. We hungrily followed her every move and kept our eyes peeled so if anything jumped out we could catch it quickly before she saw it. First we looked through the upper level, even though there was no way the creatures could've gotten up there. Then we went down into the basement. We hauled out the carpets, the mattresses, the pillows and sheets from all the rooms, but we didn't find a thing. Grandma kept searching in the bathroom and toilet, as well as the entrance hall. She didn't find anything. We breathed a little easier. Nikula looked disappointed. She dawdled a bit and was just about ready to leave when we saw it. Right on the carpeted stairs, a single little snake was happily wriggling. Where the hell had it come from? Rufi ran to grab it, but Nikula beat him to it. Her face lit up. She went out into the yard, sat down on the bench under the mulberry bush and said, "C'mere, you two."

"Auntie Nikula, we, we promise never ever to do it again." Rufi tried to break the silence in a very serious voice. My grandma paid him no attention whatsoever.

I was silent, because I knew bargaining didn't fly with her.

"Manda, what punishment do you choose?" Nikula asked me in a business-like tone, "Eating this snake alive or getting beaten with nettles?"

I watched the snake squirming in her hands and couldn't answer. I

46

waited to wake up from the nightmare, but on my right I could hear Rufi's sniveling perfectly clearly. This was no dream.

"The nettles."

"Fine."

Nikula reached toward the mulberry bush, where a rope conveniently happened to be hanging, and deftly tied me to it. Then she headed toward the garden. Rufi glanced at the gate. She caught his glance:

"Don't even think about it."

He obediently sat back down on the bench, hanging his head. We were crushed by the inevitable.

She soon returned wearing a glove on one hand and holding a fistful of nettles in the other.

"Auntie, I've gotta go home now, my mom's calling me for lunch," Rufi said timidly.

Grandma turned the huge key to the gate, slipped it into her apron and said, "You're not getting out of this. You'll stand here and watch, since you're both to blame for this mischief. That'll be your punishment."

"Please don't, Auntie Nikulaaaa, don't, don't beat her, please," Rufi was clinging to her apron. I felt a strange sense of resignation.

Nikula pushed him away and started flaying me. I was stripped to my underpants as usual. As I felt the pain, I squeezed my eyes shut so the nettles wouldn't get in them. Somewhere far away, I heard myself screaming in an unfamiliar, ugly voice that came from deep inside. I was ashamed, but it hurt like hell. Nikula was trying to outshout me.

"This'll teach you a thing or two about responsibility! This'll teach you to forget about this tomfoolery! To have respect for my hard work! To have respect for money! Where am I going to get the money to feed you now, you worthless little rat? This'll teach you to protect the family name! Yesterday's turd, you shit on my hard work," Nikula screamed, having fallen completely into a trance.

I don't remember anything after that.

When I came to, the first thing I heard was frantic pounding on the gate and Rufi's cries as he clung to the inside of it.

"Nikulaaa, open up, I'm gonna call the police," Nona, Rufi's mother, yelled from outside.

I didn't feel anything at all; the rope hardly held me. I had peed myself. Nikula, not completely recovered from her trance, tossed the nettles aside, undid the rope, threw me onto the couch on the porch, and went to open the gate.

"Are you crazy, woman?" Nona burst in and grabbed her bawling child. "I'm going to file a complaint about you, believe you me!"

"And I'll inform on that brother of yours who drags sewing machines back from the USSR and sells them. Take your little brat home before I give him a thrashing, too, for the damage they did to me." My grand-mother struggled to regain her dignity. "Let them fill your house with snakes and see how you like it!"

"But they're just kids! Don't you have any mercy?"

"I didn't touch a hair on your kid's head. Now get out of here before I thrash you as well!"

Nikula slammed the gate and bolted it. I crawled into the hall closet and hid under the coats. I had to find a way to save myself before she locked me up.

When she got back to the porch and saw that I wasn't there, Nikula flopped down heavily on the couch.

"Devil's spawn. Where the hell did she pop out of?" she whispered exhaustedly and went to look for me in the attic.

Nettle Soup

Gather only the tips of the nettles. Wash them thoroughly in water. Around a pound is enough for one quart of water. Let the water come to a boil with a pinch of salt and then add the nettles. Continue to boil uncovered for five minutes so they don't blacken. Add a bit of butter and mint and serve with feta cheese as desired.

Nettle Purée

Finely slice two pounds of nettles and cook them in one and a half cups of water for five minutes on high and five minutes on low. Brown three tablespoons of flour in a pan until it becomes golden. Add a packet of butter to the flour and gradually combine it with the nettles.

Stir the mixture until it becomes a full, thick porridge. For a more attractive presentation, it can be served with a fried egg on top and sprinkled with feta cheese, mint, and crushed walnuts.

Siemens and the Counterrevolution

I have no clear recollection of how I made it to the monastery. When I came to, I was lying in Mother Superior's cell, tightly wound in bandages. My body felt gigantic, pain radiating from everywhere. My eyes were almost swollen shut and I could hardly see Efrosinia sitting next to the bed. Her face was dark and severe. I don't know how long we had been sitting there in silence when we heard a furious pounding on the monastery gate. Voices floated toward us.

"Police! Open up!"

Mother Superior went to open the gate. I managed to sit up. Two Russian military jeeps had stopped in front of the gate and policemen were jumping out of them. Mother Superior stood on the threshold and refused to let them in. She was speaking with two hulking fellows, one of whom frequently spent the night at our house when Grandpa wasn't there. He was some bigwig from the Fatherland Front and he helped my grandma prepare her speeches; my grandma had a whole notebook full of speeches and would go around to the villages delivering them. He shoved Mother Superior out of the way and came into the courtyard.

"I'll shut down this vipers' nest of renegades," the man shouted.

"Do you have legal cause?" Mother Superior tried to remain calm.

"I am the law! I *am*, monastic scum!" he screamed.

"What are you charging us with?" Mother Superior asked.

"With the kidnapping and abuse of a minor. With the development of private business on state land with the goal of personal gain as well as plenty of other things that you'll find out for yourself in court."

"We've done no such thing."

"Yes, you have!"

Mother Superior turned around searching out the woman's voice with her dark green gaze.

"It's not true," I yelled through the window. At that moment my mother rushed through the gate. She burst into the cell, scooped me up in her arms and carried me outside.

"Wait," I yelled. "She saved me! I came here on my own," I tried to explain, but clearly for my mother at that moment the most important thing was getting me out of there.

I saw the man putting handcuffs on the nun and forcing her into the second jeep. Religion was no friend of military authority.

Everything happened very quickly after that. We didn't go back to the house at all. My mother kept me with her at the clinic until I got better. It turned out that in the meantime she had fallen in love with Major—at first I thought that was his name, but later I discovered that he was an army man being treated on her ward. After a week they released him and we left for his house in Sofia, where they got married and I started school.

Two years later, when I went back to Nesebar with my mom, I learned that they had shut down the monastery and chased away the nuns. No one knew what had happened to Mother Superior. I went to visit the monastery building, but it was deserted. Looters had ransacked the church, searching for gold hidden beneath the altar. The police had killed my grandfather's dogs and confiscated his buggy, because dogs weren't allowed to pull carts. The monastery gardens had gone to seed. The communists didn't like the monasteries and were always looking for an excuse to shut them down, so that there would be no place for crowds to gather on religious holidays and be indoctrinated with baloney about some God. During the socialist period, numerous priests and monks were killed. There could be no other faith besides belief in the Party and the proletariat's bright future.

Nikula no longer made such an effort to "educate" me or to meddle in my mother's life. She didn't dare because of the Major. Sometimes our eyes met, yet I withstood her gaze. I wasn't so afraid of her anymore. It was as if with that last beating part of her strength had been transferred to me. She felt it. And she knew that I knew it, too. I had beaten her. She would never again be that cruel to anyone. Except herself.

Some time around then, my sister Matilda was born and I was immediately assigned babysitting duties, which meant that I had to drag her around with me everywhere I went.

Otherwise, everything was as it had been. By May, the house was crawling with Czechs. The rooms had already been prepared. At dusk, the banner of Grandma's heroic life was unfurled for the tourists under the fig tree.

One late afternoon when I came back from the beach, I realized that something was going on. Nikula wasn't sitting under the fig tree telling her life story; instead, all the Czechs were crowded into the cellar, in the snake room, as we called it. I could hear their excited voices mixed with lots of shushing and the news in Czech. It was smoky. Grandma was serving coffee, water, and brandy. The Czechs were huddled around Grandpa's old Siemens radio, which he had dragged back from who knows where. Everyone wore dark worried expressions, just like Mother Superior's face as she healed me from the nettles. Grandma sent me out every hour for more brandy and soft drinks.

Counterrevolution had broken out in Czechoslovakia. Soviet and Bulgarian forces were crushing it, and people were dying on the squares of Prague. For the next week our house became something of an unofficial headquarters for information about the Prague Spring, as they would later call it. Czechs from all over Nesebar showed up.

My grandma was revitalized; surely the situation somehow reminded her of her youth as a brigadier. I sensed their fear. They didn't want to go back at all. They gathered in the courtyard and smoked in silence—a heavy, thick silence. We tiptoed around them. For the first time I felt sorry for the Czechs; until then they'd only been the puffed-up conquerors of our house to me. One by one, they packed up their luggage and left. The counterrevolution was about as effective as my snakes. As my grandmother saw them off, they cried and hugged at the gate; afterward, she moped dejectedly around the yard. She found her salvation in a new garden near the stadium that the government had given us following the Decree on Self-Sufficiency of the Population.

While our tomatoes ripened in the Nesebar sands, Jan Palach burned in Prague, Vietnam was showered with Napalm, the birth control pill now was a choice, in Paris the student chants of "It is forbidden to forbid" led to changing the constitution, and throughout America clouds of marijuana covered the hippie movement and Woodstock. It was 1969.

Exodus

After several years, Grandma and Grandpa's attempt to live out their old age together failed completely. Perhaps it was because at that point Grandpa flat-out refused to give his money to Grandma, as he had done his whole life, or perhaps it was because she was terribly jealous of him, or maybe it was because they hadn't ever really lived together and when they finally acquired their own home they realized that they had never loved each other—or at least were unable to express it. In any case, she could never forgive him for his cheerful character, which had made her fall in love with him in the first place; she could not forgive him for the abortions, the loneliness. In the end, she never managed to forgive herself for choosing the harder lot, and Grandpa could never shake off the guilt he felt toward her. They got divorced when they were both nearing eighty.

They split the floors of the house between them, and Grandma started taking Grandpa to court for various misdemeanors, including possession of the illegal pistol in the attic (she had found my hiding place). They spent yet another year in lawsuits until Boris couldn't take it anymore and sold his half of the house and garden to some other Sersemin, as Nikula put it. The sale was completely illegal; inevitably she began filing new lawsuits against the new offender, and so on and so forth until the end of her life.

Later, when I studied psychiatry, I was able to make sense of some things. The endless filing of lawsuits with the goal of proving some crackpot beliefs is defined as "querulous paranoia," while "peniaphobia" is the abnormal fear of poverty. Perhaps it's possible that the woman didn't have a bona fide disorder at all. The lawsuits were her only way of seeking some order and protection against the disintegration of her family, house, and life, which for her were one and the same thing.

With the money from his part of the house, Grandpa bought himself a beat-up old Lada, fixed up an aging house in the village of Orizare not far from the sea, and got together with Evdokia the nun. He built her a new garden and they lived together peacefully for a few years. The last time I saw him, Grandpa was in a Sofia hospital, tiny as a sparrow, in a big set of striped pajamas, whispering and sick with throat cancer.

At sixteen, after I started going to the seaside by myself, I no longer set foot in the Nesebar house. The garden was decimated by the new owner of the upper floor, and instead of oxhearts, new concrete garages ripened there, all of which were illegal. My grandma fought. The new neighbor chopped down the medlar and fig trees. She filed a complaint about them as well. Gradually the dunes were swallowed up by streets, houses, and apartment blocks. The city was advancing on all sides.

Late one evening, I passed through Nesebar with a friend to show him the house where I had grown up. We found Nikula, liberally slathered in lemon cream, reading *War and Peace* with a huge magnifying glass once again, with her mahogany ringlets utterly on end. As we went in, I called her name several times, but she was diligently sounding out the words and didn't hear me. When she finally tore her eyes from the page with great effort, she looked at me and said calmly: "Oh, is that you, Manda? Go in, go in," and sank back into the Tolstoyan mazes, as if I were still living there and had just stepped out. I'm not at all sure she even saw me as something real. Nikula passed away shortly thereafter. The house was willed to my Aunt Sara. I heard recently that she put it up for sale. She should have done that a long time ago.

Salamander

Years later, now pregnant, I'm living in a summer house in the foothills of Vitosha Mountain near the capital with my husband Arman. One day I hike up to the monastery and go into the church to light a candle. A very elderly nun is selling them. Only her eyes—cornflower blue—clearly light up her face, which is furrowed like the pit of a peach. She gives me my change and says, "It's a boy."

I look at her in astonishment, but she calmly replies, "I know."

I go to pray. Afterward, as I'm sunning myself outside in front of the church, I hear the nun's voice.

"Great shoes."

I have new, black Salamander shoes: perfect for an English missionary wife. They really are cool and mean-looking. Arman is always buying me these manly models. He doesn't like me to dress like a woman.

The voice is familiar and I can't believe my ears. I look at her.

"Sister Melania. I'm the abbess of the cloister." She gives me her hand and winks. The sea sparkles in her eyes.

After that, I go up to the monastery every day. Melania is leading its restoration. She watches over the workmen like a hawk. Her deep voice echoes in the courtyard, incongruous with her slight figure. She has a young, stern novice with her.

I give birth to a boy, Rupen.

Mother Melania baptizes us.

Part Two

Corset

Tomorrow Arman turns forty. What can I give him when he already has everything? He is a working actor and heir to a rich family.

I'll give him myself.

I go and buy a black corset with garters, stockings, and the most whorish pair of red high heels in order to erotically jumpstart our snoozing seven-year-old married life. That evening we go to another birthday party at the luxurious home of a famous poet and critic. The literary moguls hover around her. Fattened investors with connections to her husband—the minister of heavy industry—are milling around nearby. I've put on the corset, I'm not wearing panties under my luxuriant skirts, and, while we discuss the problems of hermeneutics and the third phenomenological reduction, to maintain erotic tension I discreetly masturbate on the armrest of a chair in which sits the director of the Institute for Contemporary Art.

I'm terribly tempted to strip down to my corset. Nobody realizes how close I am to acting on my fixation. These guys are obsessed with expressing themselves. I imagine how their dicks are hanging despondently in the darkness of their pants, having drained all their eroticism in the direction of tongues hopelessly entangled in perfidious analysis. Thus we get sloshed without realizing it. Especially Arman. What's gotten into him? I can't stand it any longer and pull my girlfriend into the bathroom to show her. I hike up my skirt and she just about wets herself. We giggle and whisper. People try to force the door from the outside, give up and run to piss in the courtyard. After midnight, having managed to pick fights with half the illustrious critics, which further inflames the intellectual lust of the evening, I leave with my husband, who has already staggered into his fortieth year. We brush our teeth together and gloat over some of the evening's details. He stumbles his way toward the bedroom, while I remain in the bathroom to freshen up and put the finishing touches on my plan. I come out in my full regalia. In this get-up, I leave our apartment, slam the door and go to the landing between floors where I had earlier hidden a huge bouquet of Bordeaux chrysanthemums. Flowers in hand, I ring the doorbell to complete the delivery.

I stand there in my red high heels, corset, stockings, bare ass and beaver, my top half hidden behind the Bordeaux. I deeply inhale the aroma of the graveyard—for that's how I view chrysanthemums. They are my teachers in the love of life. I prick up my ears to catch the sound of movement from inside the door. Nothing. I ring again. Silence. Just the moist graveyard fragrance and the stoicism of my red high heels.

How could I have slammed the door shut? I ring again. I can't believe it—yet another stumble into the absurd.

Arman slumbers away drunk and aesthetically exhausted from hours of verbal battles. I pull over my neighbor's coconut welcome mat and sit down gingerly as it pricks my skin. Three o'clock in the morning. He's sleeping the deep hearty sleep of a man of forty and I'm sitting bare-assed on the steps in front of my own apartment, my pussy hanging out for anyone to see.

Pounding on the door and yelling isn't an option. How could I explain to the neighbor, the wife of the chief prosecutor of the Republic of Bulgaria? The terror of humiliating myself.

Ringing the doorbell discreetly at length seems stupid and exhausting.

All of a sudden I am terribly tired from this autoerotic exertion. I just want to end these theatrics and go to bed. The last thing I remember is the feeling of my bare legs under my light-blue flannel bunny pajamas.

First ending:
The prosecutor goes to play tennis in the morning and finds me asleep in this rather undesirable pose on his very own coconut doormat, covered in Bordeaux chrysanthemums.

Second ending:
I walk down the stairs, because the elevator is broken, and inevitably pass by the bodyguard of the Head of Parliament who lives on the second floor. The bodyguard gives me his overcoat in exchange for a blowjob after which I go to my mother's, to whom I have no idea what to say.

Third ending:
I go down to the second floor, where at that very moment terrorists are kidnapping the Head of Parliament. I am the cherry on top of the whole

story, transformed into a compromising figure. I make the front page of the newspapers in my corset.

Fourth ending:
In this naughty get-up, I ring the doorbell of my third-floor neighbor, whom I find very sexy, crossing my fingers that his lover hasn't decided to sleep over.

Fifth ending:
Covered up in the bodyguard's overcoat, I go back to the home of the critic and her husband, the Minister of Heavy Industry, since they at least have a sense for the absurd. They give me a T-shirt that reads *Touch me* and we go to bed together.

Sixth ending:
Screaming and pounding, I hurl myself at our door, waking up the entire luxury apartment building, and when all the *important* neighbors start arriving, Arman sleepily opens the door, murmurs, "Oh, is it you?" and wanders back to bed.

Around noon he mischievously leans in close to me and quietly asks, "Uh, was I dreaming last night or did it seem to me that you were dressed in a rather unusual outfit?"

"Oooh, you were dreaming," I tell him, and roll over onto my other side. The corset was packed away. When I leave my husband years later, I start wearing it out to nightclubs in combination with blue Chinese coveralls, with men's patent-leather Pradas underneath, and the corset on top of everything with its garters hanging free of stockings.

Fruit Geographies

Make a dish of fruit. Peeled pears, mangoes, and lychees are the most suitable, as well as strawberries, raspberries, cherries, and melon.

Carefully arrange the slices on your lover's body and

eat them slowly. From time to time share the taste of the fruit with your lover.

This snack is refreshing and sharpens the skin's sensitivity.

Turkey

I know Arman is sleeping with Matilda, my sister.

He's been surly and anxious lately. That's a sure sign he's in love. He's left me at the summer house in Boyana with Rupen, without a car, and goes down to the city to go to the gym, to dinners, to meetings. He comes back late like a black cloud and pulls away to the other side of the bed. I hide behind yoga, culinary excesses, and walks with my son. I get up at 5 a.m. and fill pages in my journal.

"Where's my spoon? When will you ever learn to take care of me? You'll hand me the salt even before I've reached for it. There are people who know how to take care of other people. You don't see a thing. What are you looking at?" With a single gesture, Arman knocks the meal onto the floor.

Rupen asks, "Are you going to fight now?"

"Yes," we answer at the same time.

"Go play in your room," Arman says.

"You're self-centered. You only care about your writing. You use my family's wealth and make a name for yourself at my expense. But I won't put up with it anymore. I'm going to replace you!"

I clean the food off the floor, while Arman yells from the bathroom for me to set out his fucking diamond earrings before he tears off somewhere in his SUV. There are often mud stains on the passenger side.

Sometimes Matilda comes up to Boyana for dinner. She is blonde, phlegmatic, plump, with an ample bust. She loves lazing around and has the look of a person with a direct line to God and a subscription to a life at least 300 years long. It's fun when Matilda comes to the house. She drags some gay guy along with her, who devours Arman with his eyes. He prances back and forth, basking in all that attention, carefree, ready to entertain. He spoonfeeds Matilda black caviar and regales us with stories.

The next day, he is withdrawn again. I have the feeling that I'm living with two different people and that I put up with the morose one in hopes that the sunny one will come out again tomorrow. I ask him, "Why are you doing this to me?"

"I need you," he says. "You're necessary so I can flirt with other women. I can only do it in your presence. Otherwise I scare them and they run away."

"OK, then I'll flirt, too."

"No, no, you can't. You will always remain My Wife."

One day, while I'm complaining to Matilda on the phone that I can't go on living like this, she cuts me off with the question: "Well, what are you still doing there?"

At that moment, my body realizes that she is sleeping with Arman. There is something in the question's intonation, something in her sincere astonishment that, despite everything that is going on I'm still in that bed. *For Christ's sake, won't you finally get the hell out of there so I can lie down in it?*

That night, I stand by the window, stripped at once of both my families. I don't let on that I know. I plan my escape from this trap. I desperately need funds. I go to a casting call for hosts on a French radio network that is opening a local station in Sofia. A week later they call to tell me that I got the gig. Arman is furious. He can't stand not having me around the house. He doesn't want me to work. He wants me to be dependent on him. I start at 3:30 every morning, translating news that comes over the French wires, and reading it on the information bulletin at 8:30, after which I prepare reports for the next day until two in the afternoon.

My salary is huge, but I don't have time to spend it. Christmas time rolls around. I shop like crazy. Arman hates me having my own money. I'm late getting home. The house is dark, Arman is sitting on the couch. He stands up and puts the keys to the house and the car in his pocket. He takes my bags of purchases and throws them out the window and they scatter into the street. He sits down to play the piano. I feed our son. Arman reads him a bedtime story.

We meet again in the darkened living room.

I say, "I'm not going to take this anymore."

Arman kicks me in the shins with his pointy shoe. He drags me by my hair all around the house.

As my scalp is parting ways with my skull, the thought blazes in my head: *If I don't defend myself tonight, this will go on forever.* I take advantage of a loosened grip and rake my nails across his face. I leave three deep bloody scratches on both sides of his nose. Arman touches the trickling blood and blanches. He gets sick at the sight of blood. He goes to the bathroom to inspect the damage.

My heart stops. I run to the kitchen and look for the meat cleaver. When he jumps out from around the corner of the hallway enraged, I chase him through the house. Arman is laughing and hopping across the couch and chairs, hiding behind doors, but there is fear in his eyes. He barges into Rupen's room and cowers behind the bed. Dawn has broken outside. Rupen sits up in bed, blinking sleepily.

"What are you doing?"

"Your mother wants to kill me."

I leave my son's room.

It is already light.

Arman goes into the bedroom and locks the door.

I sit down on the couch with the cleaver in my lap. Is this real? Is this my life?

Usually such clashes are followed by a month of silence, during which our pets die. Last time, the dog died.

Tomorrow is Christmas Eve. We go over to Arman's parents' place. His mother looks at me, frightened. "Manda, what did you do to him? How could you?" I sit down at the table like a convicted killer. Shocked and awed, they bring me food. His father tries to smooth everything over with jokes. It's warm. It smells of

Dried Red Peppers Stuffed with Beans

Soak a pound of ripe green beans overnight. In the morning, boil them over low heat until they are completely soft. Drain out the liquid and set it aside. Pour a third of a cup of olive oil in a frying pan and sauté three large onions until translucent. Add three tablespoons of paprika and a handful of mint. Immediately add the drained green beans and a teaspoon of salt. Take thirty dried red peppers, which you have soaked in water in advance until they have expanded. Fill them with the bean mixture. Place them in an open pan or a big pot, clay if possible. Pour another third of a cup of olive oil over them, plus two cups of the water the beans had

boiled in, and bake them in a moderately hot oven for
around 40 minutes.

Christmas Eve. Awaiting a beginning. After the Bad Arman has been exhausted, the Good Arman returns. He hands me a long red envelope with a rose drawn on it. On the back is written: *"To my dearest wife, to spend it on whatever and however she sees fit, to feel free to make art, to enjoy life and to go to her favorite city."* Inside is a wad of British pounds and a ticket to London. That's how it is after every brawl. I get a bribe. Sometimes I take them. I play the game. But not this time. As we're leaving, my mother-in-law surreptitiously shoves a box of pearls into my hand. More pearls. I have enough already, I say.

She whispers, "If something happens, if you're out of money." Unshaken female solidarity has bound me to her ever since I joined that family. Even in the very beginning she warned me: "Don't marry my son! Please, he has a terrible nature. We are in love with suffering. He has inherited all of my Armenian madness." But who was listening then?

The holidays are like a bobsled track. Everyone hurls themselves down it trustingly, bringing with them all their hopes for a miracle and their lack of any choice.

The next day is Christmas and we have been invited to a turkey dinner by the architects Konstantin and Irina Filipov. The Filipovs' *puyka s kesteni* is a culinary event that is a topic of conversation for weeks before and after Christmas. They are a weighty Sofia family with style and traditions. The family tree is full of five generations of doctors, lawyers, and generals, which now has come down to Konstantin and Irina's family with their twin sons, who were studying law and medicine in Paris. These identical savages have been growing before my eyes for years, rowdy and tough, they were on the rowing team, wore ripped jeans, didn't bathe, and regularly skipped school. Their fearsome mother, who had exhausted all of their resources trying to force them into the family mold, laid into them directly with her clogs, since her hands ached from swatting their bony frames.

Arman was especially devoted to their grandmother, Irina's mother, Mrs. Tsvetana Galileeva. The wife of a gynecologist, she had never worked a day in her life. She was a petite grande dame in simple black dresses with an obligatory string of pearls around her neck. She had stood behind her husband for half a century and had brought up, educated, and properly married off four daughters. Mrs. Tsvetana had her bridge club on Thursday with other biddies and never stepped outside without a veiled hat and gloves to fit the season. You could call Mrs. Tsvetana at five o'clock in the morning to ask her what to do with a dead man right after he had passed away, or what to do on the forty-day anniversary of his passing or what to do with the deceased's clothes, for example. She knew all there was to know about Bulgarian customs: the proper number of dishes on Christmas Eve, rituals for the church calendar, juicy stories about Sofia's past. Mrs. Tsvetana was a walking book of customary law, both contractual and civil, she had mastered accounting, worldly gossip, managing a family budget and real estate, and all those other less-than-obvious tricks for keeping a family in order. Once I asked her what was the secret to creating tradition in that family and why marriages in it ended only when death got in the way. Tsvetana gave me a mischievous look: "The men work and then hand their wallets over to the women, because they know best what the family needs."

While Mrs. Tsvetana smears the *puyka s kesteni*—turkey with chestnuts—with honey and lemon as a finishing touch, we find ourselves on the slippery slide of the holidays.

I'm wearing a caramel-colored, Renaissance-style, floor-length velvet tunic, from beneath which peek the light-blue sleeves of a dress with a hand-knitted lace collar. A velvet caramel-colored hat with a decoration on the front sits on my head. Arman is in black Yves Saint Laurent, with six scratch marks on his face. At nine o'clock sharp we arrived unabashed at the home of our stunned hosts, who are tactful enough not to ask any questions.

Two fireplaces have been lit in the enormous living room. The woodwork has been shined with scented oil, the pink Persian carpets are thick and soft, with carefully combed fringe, the porcelain and crystal glitter in the darkness of the heavy cupboards. Political, religious, and all manner of worldly moguls have been invited. A white Persian cat strolls proudly among them, with a golden medallion around its neck. Fluffy Irina is in her element, entertaining the guests and ordering around the servant girl who carries platters in and out. I settle into an armchair by the fireplace, thankful for the warmth and security that inhabits this home. I feel as if I have just been rescued from a ship sinking in an icy ocean. They are giving me one more chance at life. Pleasantly keyed up, everyone awaits the appearance of the turkey, which will be carried in by Mrs. Tsvetana. Her white coiffed hair, her aristocratic face and frail body are incongruous with the strength with which she carries the platter holding the wondrous *puyka*. The chatter dies down. Everything is now centered around the turkey. Konstantin carves it deftly. The guests take the seats Irina points out to them.

I've been assigned to a spot in a nook near the library, along with Mrs. Tsvetana and the twins.

Arman is seated to Irina's right, across from a presidential candidate and his would-be VP. Everyone falls silent over their plates. Only exclamations and comments on the wine are heard.

The twins are in their college blazers. We have a lighthearted conversation about their studies and life in Paris. Their grandmother shares details about the house in Mare that she has recently bought for the students and where she has recently been spending quite a bit of time keeping an eye on them. I listen with relief to accounts of such prosperity.

The *puyka* has thin, crispy skin, the meat is tender, swimming in a mixture of apples and chestnut puree. I close my eyes and sigh to better take it in. The taste of the meat starts out innocently, steeped in the sweetness of the chestnuts and sent on its way by the delicately astringent tang of the apples. I savor it and don't want to dress up this sensation in words, yet etiquette prevails. It is only proper to acknowledge this culinary masterpiece, into which Mrs. Tsvetana has poured all of her ample talents. I take a sip of wine and say: "Your *putka* is very tasty, Mrs. Tsvetana!"

I freeze. *This is a dream. It must be a dream. Please tell me this is a dream.* I look at the *puyka*. I said "*putka*"! I told my host that her cunt is very tasty! I don't breathe. I watch the twins out of the corner of my eye—they are holding their plates in mid-air, looking at their grandmother. I glance at Tsvetana. Unfazed, she is eating, her knees pressed properly together, carefully watching what is happening on her plate. Perhaps she didn't hear me. But both those morons surely did. Sounds of choking and growling come from their direction. They are as red as the fireplace screen glowing from the flames. The next instant, they toss their plates to the floor and with a muffled roar rush out of the library. From the hallway to the bathroom the shouts of people taking a breath for the first time can be heard. I sit there across from Tsvetana, my eyes nailed to my plate. I would kill to be in the bathroom with the twins, rolling around amidst the towels with them, or at least in the hallway, anywhere but here with this unflappable woman. Apologizing to her isn't an option. Centuries pass, I'm not the one sitting there holding a plate when I see the Persian cat in my lap devouring a piece of my turkey. Tsvetana's quick hands scoop the cat off my lap and I hear her clear voice:

"Yes, it is very delicious. But, Manda, you haven't eaten anything at all."

From very close up, I see her blue eyes, filled with irony and severity.

At that moment Irina twitters something about coffee and cake being served in the other salon. Mrs. Tsvetana excuses herself and goes to help. I rush down the hallway and sink into the minks on the coatrack. Heavily perfumed skins. I'm suffocating. I grab my ermine wrap and leave the Filipovs' home. Only when I reach the street do I take a breath. An icy Christmas evening. I'm on duty at the radio station. I have two hours before my morning shift begins. I slowly walk past the monument to the Soviet army. Snow falls in large flakes. Somewhere up above they are beating big fluffy quilts. I walk slowly, letting the snowflakes melt on my face. The intersection near the courthouse is quiet. There are no cars. Everyone is at home, hunkered down around their turkeys. The only thing moving are the billboards at the intersection. Instead of the usual ads they are showing porn. Shot at a distance and close up. All kinds. Hetero. Homo. Back and forth. Back and forth. I watch the movements, the shapes and the orifices. Warm pink flesh. Completely vulnerable there in the cold, at the intersection. I stand there, aroused by the scale. By what these huge, sweaty people are doing next to the cold buildings. The wind jostles me, blowing open my ermine wrap. It is strangely quiet. Only the snow moans under my feet. Every billboard along the way tugs at me with its S&M, transvestites, hardcore porn. I'm nearing the studio. The city is deserted. Who will I be preparing the news for, now that the inhabitants have disappeared? All the billboards are broadcasting porn channels. There's no need to buy or sell anything. Porn.

On a blind wall directly across from the glass windows of the radio station, a huge neon sign blinks: I SEE YOU, BUT YOU DON'T SEE ME!

I go into the dark studio. I take off the wrap, put on some coffee and watch the sign. Shadows of snowflakes and letters roll down my face. I SEE YOU, BUT YOU DON'T SEE ME!

I see you but you don't see me, you don't see mee, you don't seee meee.

I start singing along, letting the world murmur in my headphones.

Over the holidays, fighting has continued in the Gaza Strip. Pope John Paul arrived on a visit to ...

In the morning, when my co-workers show up, I tell them the story about the *puyka*. They squeal, roll around on the rug and race to clip out turkey recipes and scrawl in a "t" from the pre-Christmas newspapers: Cunt with Sauerkraut, Cunt Bismarck, Imperial Cunt, Stuffed Cunt with Apples, Cunt with Stuffing, Baked Cunt with Grape Leaves, American cunts are dangerous, "How to Raise a Cunt," and so on, until the whole window between the sound booth and studio is plastered with recipes for cunt. The sound engineer can barely see through all those cunts.

That's how news is read during the first month of the new 1996. Straight from the source.

Turkey with Chestnuts

Tsvetana Galileeva's secret is injecting the turkey with a syringe of melted butter so it is juicy, albeit quite caloric.

Ingredients: one turkey (around ten pounds), one small onion, a half-pound of shelled chestnuts, 3.5 ounces of foie gras (duck or goose), salt and black pepper to taste, three green apples, one stick of butter.

Once the turkey is cleaned and washed, coat it liberally both outside and inside with salt and butter.

For the stuffing: Saute the onion, chestnuts and the chopped-up foie gras in butter. Peel the green apples and steam them until soft and make them into a puree. Add black pepper. Fill the turkey with this stuffing.

Sew the turkey shut and place it in a pan. Pour a bit of water in and cover the whole pan with foil.

Bake the turkey in the oven at a moderate heat for two and a half to three hours, taking it out every 40 minutes to add a little more water and to coat it with butter. At the end, remove the foil and put the pan back in the oven for 15 minutes to make the skin crispy. Before serving, coat the turkey with a mixture of honey and lemon.

Fathers and Mothers

Get up and enter your life—that's what I tell myself. *So what if your stomach hurts. You've poured yourself into this bed. You can't live it out lying down, pretending to be in it, complaining, while your life slips away little by little. No books are going to save you.* I get up. I'm going to write down my dream now. But I'm cold. *Get dressed quick and run over to the desk before you've forgotten it.* I feel like drinking tea and I remember that writer who started writing before the water for his coffee boiled. I put on mine for tea and keep asking myself how can I not have a single warm friendly sweater for these fucking days, when I take at least five hot baths, stand around in front of Open Societe foundation, asking for money for my magazine *Post Scriptum*. I want to create a magazine about female spirituality and integration between the sexes. I try to bring us into conversation with men. In search of that lost language while puddles form beneath me, that's how hard it's raining. I go on foot and don't give a shit. Cars stall in the flood. All the better—a disaster! Then off to another foundation, wet as I am. Good thing I remembered: the kid! I've got a kid. Rupen is the only ray of light on that day. I pick him up from the pool and there as we mothers jostle, I stare at the coach's tits and ask myself whether I'm not a latent lesbian after all, because I'm fine with an absent man. I keep thinking it over on the way to the foundation, with all men absent, but then again it's never been good for me with a woman, there's always something not quite right, some taste of cardboard. I have a peculiar need for distance from a man, but afterward I tell myself *That's what you think, but when he left how badly you wanted to tell him stay, but that's never going to happen, because you don't believe he'll stay or he'll leave precisely because you're begging him.* But it's nice being surrounded by tenderness, so better to break down that spitefulness, to get rid of it, because the hatred gets in my way. That needle in the ear. I'll admit it, I'm always attracted to passive men, as feminine as women, but I always choose the bad boys. Is there no end in sight? Sometimes I simply can't stand it here anymore. I pray: anything but the waterworks right now. The sky has bottomed out. That's how I want to cry. To have a sweet little cry, to warm my soul. I don't dare. I avoid the puddles and delight in my sturdy Get-a-Grip shoes with their steel toes. I am finally at home in them; at least my shoes are OK and who really gives a shit that it's raining, I've got my scarf, also English, a brown cap *contre ventes et marées.* On my way back I see little figures painted on a garage dancing in a line, threaded on some stake through their stomachs.

I'm not waiting for anyone to come back, to leave, to stay. I only know that I am trying to get up and to enter myself, but I can't. It's so awful there, it's so crammed full, foreign, cold. They hate me there, too. Some characters have moved in there and all they do is judge, they size me up, they want to cut my hair, they buy me too-tight shoes. They don't want me to write. They scream *Get rid of that crappy form already, you can't say anything new with it anyway,* that I'm crazy, that I don't even have a single decent sweater—no warm friend—and that it's my own fault that a good guy is never going to turn up, that, in fact, I don't want him, I'm never going to love myself, that I adore being punished, being hit, being humiliated. They tell me that I've deserved it ever since I was little. Others can always sense it and there's always somebody to torment me in the pool. After practice they corner me in the deep end and hold me under in shifts, but I don't dare complain. They say *Come on!* And I take up my place for torture.

Who said there wouldn't be any victims in this story?

Oh, how I'd like to paint bright pictures not nailed down to anything!

Yeah, but I've got a big fat cork to spit out! Only her head is still above water, you'll have to put up with it, dear relatives, it can't be helped. I go to cook furiously, I make flavor and colors with breath. My mother comes in, looks at me with the slightly glassy stare of someone who has just floated up from the abyss, roams through the house, ostensibly straightening up, but in fact she'd really like to sit down and have a chat—a whole life of empty words, sitting in that which has just leaked out, bundling up, sucking the past and the future dry! Terrifying! You should've. You must! We stand there. God forbid we take a step forward, God forbid we sprout wings: they beat us where our wings should be! It's very painful. The wings are delicate and unprotected, that's precisely why down sprouts there, feathers burst forth, but look: the doorbell rings and the father enters! Now we've got both mommy and daddy. If I can manage to get them in focus, I'll film them. Together! There they are sitting there, looking at each other—crushed, without being fighting cocks, destroyed by inertia.

"How are you?" he asks her.

"You're living the high life," she says, "while I'm working myself to death and as a reward you see what she writes about me in her books—not a single good word."

"Come on now, big deal," the father laughs.

Then she's supposedly talking to him, but manages to say that my house is cold, that it isn't cozy, that I just run here and there.

He defends me: "She's a smart girl. I put her on a pedestal" and asks me, "Aren't you gonna give me any cash for taxes?"

She lashes out. "Of all the nerve! Don't give him anything," she says. I give him some.

"That's not enough . . ." he says and rubs the bills together. He gets up and yells, "Yooohooo!"

They laugh, my beaten-down, non-fighting cocks, beaten black and blue even before the battle by some other beaten-down ones, and I say to myself: God, I'm going to throw these two out, so insecure, selfish, cold, careless, aged children who have come to give, but have forgotten, they've never known how. I already wish they had never come and for me not to be. He leaves. She stays to keep sucking away. I cry and yell: "You want a book, right, you want to read, you ask—'Are you writing anything? Your stuff is genius! Why have you stopped writing?'—You want me to have a family, too: For him to be artistic. Rich. Sensitive and cool. And to watch me on TV. To hear me on the radio. To read interviews, to be famous, to definitely and irreversibly hold power! To be successful! To conquer the world! To be the shit and, if possible, to organize my closets like a busy bee. For everything to be clean! To always have something rising in the oven, when I'm not talking over there. To smell of starched apple pies and a child, children, because I've got to have at least one more.

Noooooooooooooooooooooooooooooooooooooooooooooooooooo, I can't take any more.

Someone badmouths me and out of the fear that the guilty party may be you, you badmouth me in turn.

Don't you have that membrane called love, desperate love, which believes? Believes in me? Out of that, out of all of that, what have you done, what have you achieved? Where is the opening onto these desires so I can plug them up and surrender? So I can fall asleep in the mud, a drunken whore, unknown to anybody. So I can devour that hellish piston, which chases me away from everywhere and from myself.

So I can put on a cotton-print dress and sit down on the doorstep with an apple. Yes.

Apple Tart

Prepare a crumbly dough from one and a half cups of flour, one stick of melted butter, a pinch of salt and a tablespoon of water. Spread the dough on the bottom of a greased and floured pan and cover it with slices of three large sour apples, peeled. Prepare cream from: a half cup of sugar whipped with a quarter stick of butter, two eggs and a pinch of cinnamon, mixing it until it whitens. Pour the cream over the apples. Bake the tart in a medium-hot oven. When it is ready, cut a slice of the aroma and put it away for days when you urgently need to create coziness.

Paris

I'm in Paris, studying cultural programming at Radio France International and using every spare second to decipher this unknown world. Being absolutely anonymous has its advantages. I can think up whatever I want. I'm unfettered. I quickly have to become my own father and mother. I adopt myself.

I look around the city.

A truly hot Parisian day, when there's almost no boundary between the body's outside and inside. I drink all kinds of cold things on the café terraces, dip my feet into the lazy Seine, gape at the shop windows, exhibits, and Japanese furniture stores. Good thing that the city pulls back along the river. Sprawling on the stone parapets, I forget myself in the unbelievable space, I breathe with huge lungs and open sails, I cruise on a yacht toward the ocean.

Paris is a monster. It sniffs out the monster in me and, frenzied, together they rush ahead, backward, up and around, ever hungry for new things. I drag myself to the Pompidou, where there's a Surrealism exhibit. I'm doubtful as to how much of a revolution can be displayed in a gallery.

I imagine how many floors I have to traipse through and plop myself down on the cobblestones a few meters from the one-legged clock in front of the museum.

This is one of the liveliest places in Paris. In the morning you can play the intellectual here in one of the nearby café-libraries, where, while *on prend le café,* as the French say, you have at your disposal all the latest books, including the literary press with all its vanity and gossip. That is, if you're in the mood to play at being anything at all that early. It's enough just to close your eyes and let the scents carry you away. Mmmm, here are the chocolate-filled croissants, there are the brioche. From the side streets waft the smells of every delicious dish in the world, instantly taking me back to Grandma's stove. Thus transformed into a taste bud, you swoop down on the waiter who is freshening up the sidewalk in front of the restaurant with a bucket of water.

The water in Paris in the morning forms rivers along the sidewalks that carry away the dust and leave in their wake an inimitable freshness—the day is beginning! The day in this city, which has gathered so many people and so much energy, lies ahead.

The late afternoon grants me long sun. The square in front of the Pompidou is the place where you can always find someone to entertain you if you're bored: fire eaters, strongmen breaking chains, mimes painted in bronze and frozen like statues, jugglers, magicians, and singers. And, of course, thousands of pigeons.

I lie there, absolutely given over to this Babylon. I watch the pigeons battling for seeds at the clock's foot and notice a bald pigeon with a patch of dried blood on his head, trying to climb up the sloping brass pedestal. His little red legs energetically gather speed and he manages to reach about halfway up, but after that he slides back down, where several of his vicious brethren peck at his injured head.

The pigeon stubbornly insists on walking up. Failing, he gets pecked back down at the bottom. As I'm wondering why he doesn't use his wings to fly, I notice three Indians passing by the clock: two men and a beautiful woman. She is nearest to the clock. As they pass by the base, the woman gracefully bends down in her orange sari, scoops up the pigeon with two fingers, helps him climb up the pedestal, and calmly continues on her way.

I watch.

Existence teaches me its lessons:

"If you have wings and don't use them, they'll kick you down at the bottom."

And what's more: "If you follow your path, you'll always find helpers."

Red Dress

One morning I see it very clearly: velveteen the color of clotted blood, floor-length, fitted at the waist and flared below, with fifty small, covered buttons on the front.

I am hopelessly in love with a man from whom I am separated by oceans, continents, and my own indecisiveness.

Given this abundance of libido and its lack of an object, everything around is red. Vitosha Mountain is a gigantic tit, the blossoming apricots are vaginas, but depression is black.

The velveteen arrives all the way from Taiwan, and my favorite seamstress and I start creating—a tried-and-true remedy against depression. I stand in front of the mirror for a fitting. We giggle, she coos over me. A month later I have a blood-red cardinal's dress.

To save my family, I transform my love for this man into a dress, I write a book, build two matchless houses, and study psychoanalysis.

I don't have the guts to leave my husband. A heavy patriarchal fossil is stuck in my throat. I am afraid of the responsibility to destroy. Of being a bad girl.

This is how culture is born.

I show up in Lugano for the final exam to receive my diploma as a bodily oriented psychotherapist. At the very beginning of my studies, my Swiss professor asks me: "Manda, why are you here?"

"Because I put up with situations that make me unhappy, yet I can't decide to put an end to them. Because in the morning my self-confidence is subzero, while by lunchtime I've conquered the world, and in the evening I'm back down at rock bottom. Because I want to feel good in my own skin, because I want to be able to stand up for myself . . . because I want love."

"And what are you willing to give for that?" the professor asks me with a mischievous smile.

I keep digging.

We're doing the five movements of the neo-Reichian practice (planning, submission, seduction, aggression, and reality check). These are models for human communication which we are born with, but which we forget in the process of our "education." Tonight is seduction. We are practicing the art of attracting others. I put on my blood-red dress, with my trusty corset underneath, along with fishnet stockings, garters, and red high heels. I'm going to knock them dead. My turn comes. There's no music. There are forty fellow students, their chairs lined up in a half-circle, with the professor's teaching assistant across from them in the center. I start dancing in front of each one, my strategy being to seduce each one personally. But she stops me. I'm supposed to stand in the back facing her and to seduce them all at once through self-seduction. Jerked out of my plan, I freeze up. Now there's the inconvenience of having plans for you. To make matters worse, at my every move the assistant tells me how I should be doing it, how it isn't right. What's the matter with me anyway? Why am I so uptight?

I want to sit down, but this is part of the test. The idea that I have no choice paralyzes me all the more and I barely manage to budge, wanting to sink into the ground out of shame. That gangly bitch who doesn't even know how to begin to shake her ass hollers something at me about being more fluid.

I can't move. My mind is blank. Only afterward (always afterward) did it occur to me that I could've taken off that dress and been left only in my lingerie. I could have imagined something that would have brought on the sense of seduction. I could've done a lot of things, but when they stick you right in the trauma, you're only as old as you were when they first shamed you—four, for example. So at four, what ideas?—what erotica?—if they'd cut you down right when you were beginning to blossom? Shame, burning shame, awkwardness and the desire to hide, like in the poem about the big bear's long tail. Like a red scarecrow, I hang in front of everybody's stares for ages. Nothing remains of my self-confidence, while that magnificent dress and all the accessories are an utter mockery. I would've been better off in my dungarees. When I finally sit down I have the feeling that they've just raped me.

The assistant attacks the next student in the same way, but she is far gutsier. She tells the assistant to shut her mouth. This is her seduction and she'll do it as she sees fit. I see how she's able to defend herself, while I can't, paralyzed by the feeling of helplessness and lack of choice, by the fear that they'll fail me. The exercise ends; everybody is partying. I stand aside in my red dress. How pointless its beauty is. I go to take it off. I dress entirely in black—I put on my manliest pants, my black men's Prada shoes and a black sweater. That gives me security and protection. I attack the assistant. I scream something about empathy and about the lack of love, I ask her whether she really loved me so much so as to allow herself to humiliate me like that and I ask her what, in fact, is her problem with seduction? Why doesn't she go work it out, rather than project it onto me and traumatize me all over again? I'm not just her puppet here I remind her. All words, but so late in coming, yet that's how I wish I had erupted at the moment it was happening. Nevertheless, I've made progress, because before, following such an incident, I would've composed monologues on the subject for a year afterward. I really ripped into her. The next day she apologizes to me, but the scene has unblocked such a river of pain within me that I can't stop crying for two days

The pain is solitary. Unbearable. On the other hand, it dilutes me in some strange way. I don't know what this grief is, but I don't prevent it from pouring out. Later, a Zen teacher tells me that what hurts is the ego; the soul doesn't feel a thing.

I pass the fucking test. For some time I look into what prevented me from being self-seductive. It has something to do with unconditional love, love for one's self, with internal spaces. I try this and that.

I don't dare go near the red dress for a long time.

House

No one has lived in No. 13 for a long time.
By day only the wind whirls leaves around the statue by the entrance.
After sundown, behind the façade sunk in ivy, strange noises can be heard, music.
The bogs of the windows come to life.
If he gathers the courage to peer through them, the tempted passerby will see in the huge living room all those who have ever inhabited this house.

I'm writing in the kitchen of the Kovachevitsa house in the Eastern Rhodope Mountains. I have my own house. I accept it with fear. So huge, so empty, so beautiful. The bells along the veranda and the nearby trees gnaw the silence with every gust of wind. For years, I've been collecting the bells from various eastern temples, presents from friends. That's what they call it in the village: the House of Bells. Barely clinging to the steep slope, several levels of flagstone courtyards stitch it onto the hill. The fourteen-meter-long veranda is a room without walls with a long table for weddings, which flows into a huge canopy bed, so that those who have left the feast prematurely can lie down and still be part of the action. At the very front in the corner of the veranda stands a tall chimney—this way the observer has the hill, along with fire and rain, at their disposal. The river can be heard running through the valley below.

My husband and I have built two houses, one on the seaside and this one in the Rhodopes. He imagines us hiding ourselves away under the colossal roofs, the crystal glasses, the horses and dogs, servants, the silence, private tutors for our son. He wants me all to himself. He's jealous of the world, of my writing, of the breath I take. He tells Rupen: "I found the most beautiful and talented woman to give birth to you." He hates every sign of joy and freedom in me and desires me passionately only when I am in the depths of despair. But I can't imagine us locking ourselves up in these castles. We split up right when we were supposed to start living in them. He took the seaside one, I took our son and the house in the medieval village in the mountains.

Anything you put that much into soon turns into a trap. Housetraps. Now, two years after our separation the house is terrifyingly quiet. I'm writing the insert for a CD of contemporary music. It will be called *House No. 13*. I'm writing about myself, as always.

In front of the fireplace, they listen to some childless auntie playing the
    piano, waiting for touches under the table, all aflame,
in the glasses—heavy blood
from the eastern, western, southern slope.
In the pauses the rustling of the servants, the children's quickened breath by
the crack in the door, barefoot beneath their nightgowns.

I'm writing. I'm sniffling. A fire is burning in the oven the height of the table. I look at it and remember how I dreamed of having just such a fire, such a table and of writing there, protected. Now I'm writing and grieving. Could grief simply be a habit, some ordinary husk flaking off me, long since unnecessary, yet more certain than joy?

The house is empty. Empty of family—children, adults, and animals. The family.

Until some train barges into this story,
all wrapped in steam.
By the fire, amidst lost gloves and tear-soaked silk kerchiefs,
remains only the Hen with her sewn-up eye.
She swings her three-toed shoe,
her gaze fixed on the departing ones.
Every blink of her single eyelid
counts off the change of the seasons.

At that moment there is a terrifying bang. I don't understand what's going on. When I come to my senses, the whole kitchen is filled with firebrands and thick smoke. I stand there, stunned; I don't know for how long. Someone inside me fills buckets with water, screams!

I stomp, pour, and extinguish. The stone slab in front of the mouth of the oven has exploded, filling the whole room with red-hot rocks, embers, and burning wood.

The house cannot stand this pain. My feeling of guilt. It can't stand me. It wants to kill me.

Christos

To part with something that has long been slowly dying requires much strength. Much more strength.

I mentally rehearse leaving Arman. I often go the apartment I inherited from my grandfather. I renovate it to serve as the editorial office for *Post Scriptum*. I go and sit in this space, which is now new to me, and try to imagine how I might live there. I've knocked out all the walls. There is only one separate room left. A large space with a fireplace in the middle and a futon. White walls, oak floors, and windows down to the ground, looking out toward the birch trees.

A heavy silence reigns at home. Arman and I pass each other like strangers. He makes me sign some documents rejecting any claims on properties acquired during our marriage. I tell him to take everything and just leave me the Kovachevitsa house. I don't have any strength to fight him. I can barely drag myself to work at the radio.

One day I come down with a nasty case of cystitis and go to get tested. The lab tech, a Serbian woman with quite a mouth on her, barges into the room waving the test results, and starts screaming at me.

"Hey, bitch, have you been starvin' yourself for thirty days or what? I'm gonna kill you!"

I look at her in bewilderment.

My urine is full of acetone, as much as in people who have completely decayed.

I had no idea that I was in such bad shape. That I hadn't been eating. That I hadn't been sleeping. That I was dying.

Clearly, I'm much more ready to die than to get up and leave.

I am well versed in the typical Balkan mold: "Put up with it, my girl, put up with it!" is the motto of every woman who has brought up daughters in these latitudes.

"Are ya gonna live or die?" The Serbian woman waves the sheets full of molecules over my head.

"I'm going to live."

I get up, go home, pack two suitcases with only the most necessary things, grab my son and take refuge in the empty editorial office.

And with that, my energy is sapped. I'm in a stupor for two weeks. The front door of my apartment is like a theater stage—with various characters entering and exiting—friends, relatives. The hardwood floor has swelled from the painting. My father, in his typical style, reads me the riot act: "What have you done to your grandfather's home? What are these rolling hills here?" and leaves, slamming the front door.

That's his way of holding me together.

My sister shows up in denim overalls and a set of monkey wrenches. She drags me out to shop for household appliances and handily starts installing them.

All this commotion is a good thing, it doesn't leave me much time to get depressed.

We dig through a few attics and basements and find wondrous old things—a cherry wood, Secessionist-style wardrobe, an old couch that we split in two to make chairs. I make Rupen a bureau by stacking up four cardboard boxes that I've cut little doors into—the biggest box on the bottom is for bigger things, while the littlest one on top is for underwear. Several months go by. Rupen and I create a new life. He is upset that we don't have a TV and a whole slew of other things. I'm worried about how to smoothly transition from the standard of living he had gotten used to and our present reality. "Don't worry about those things, they'll come in their own good time—the most important thing is to have a place to be yourself and to feel at home." That what our old family doctor tells me. I already have such a place. Despite the fact that for a few years, I keep catching myself glancing fearfully at the front door, expecting it to open and Arman to come bursting in. My boundaries have been so completely punctured that it takes me time to get used to my freedom. A freedom so huge that it's frightening. Since there's no pressure anymore, it often takes on the form of a bottomless, icy emptiness.

The fire in the fireplace does a good job warming things up. I don't have any wood, so I gather some from two nearby construction sites. Almost every night I go out with a sack looking for unused boards and scrap lumber.

I can't sleep. I can't write. The fire dies out and I go out for wood again. Whenever I pass by the apartment building next door, one window on the ground floor is always lit up, with the shades drawn. I'm tempted to go over to see whom my insomniac brother-in-arms is, but I don't have the guts. I'm even a little annoyed. Doesn't anybody around here sleep?

Gradually all the trappings of ordinary family life give way to the craziness of two people in puberty—Rupen has just entered his, while I'm going through my own late version of it.

We write each other notes right on the wall in the enormous space that we use for everything. No more daily cooking. We eat sandwiches. My son's friends and mine come over and since we don't have any furniture, we roll around on pillows on the floor.

I'm putting together the first issue of *Post Scriptum*. I publish it with George Soros' money, through his Open Society Foundation in support of the democratic process in Bulgaria.

I have a meeting with Leo, the magazine's designer, in the courtyard of the theater academy.

We're hunkered down over our layout, each with a glass of crème-de-menthe and soda, when a young man with tousled chestnut hair comes over to us. He stands while exchanging a few words with Leo. I lift my head to look at him.

At that moment, everything stops.

I look at him and hear someone inside me say calmly: *He's the one.*

What purity. He's not of this world. As if he has just left a monastery. A pale face, dark green eyes and a slender, proud figure. With that radiance he would later play all the saints, knights, and men of honor in international cinema. He says goodbye to Leo.

No, the voice in me screams, *don't go. Stay!*

That same day I run across him three times downtown—his loose green shirt fluttering.

A week later I spot him at a nightclub. I'm with a noisy group, seriously high and drunk. Again the same feeling of closeness to this young man. I lie in wait for him behind a pillar and kiss him. Taken aback by such boldness, both of us get lost in the dancing crowd.

The next day, I hang around the courtyard of the theater academy with a glass of dark green crème-de-menthe, hoping to catch a glimpse of him.

I'm chatting with Anna, who I know from my class on Chinese poetry, when the young man from the nightclub passes by and greets her familiarly.

"Do you know each other?" I ask her.

"Yes."

"I really like him. I'm crazy about him. What's his name?"

"Christos."

"How do you know him?

"He's my son," she says. "He's studying here at the theater academy."

My heart sinks into my shoes. I pull myself together and invite them to lunch.

So, here we are at lunch—mother, son, and me.

Christos is looking at me unfazed from beneath his chestnut locks and listening distractedly to my conversation with Anna about our favorite Eastern teacher.

I feel I'm losing him and say: Tonight there's a talk with David Lynch at the Red House, do you want to go?

Thank God, the mother is busy. Christos nods.

I say, "I'll wait for you at seven in front of the house."

Each of us heads off somewhere in the hot June afternoon.

The sun is merciful around seven, when I drag over a chair from the nearby café and take up a strategic position at the corner of the Red House, so I can see both directions from which my angel might appear.

A half-hour goes by. There is no sign of him.

I sit.

Are you crazy to keep sitting here like that in the void when it's obvious he's not coming.

But a voice in me says: I have all the time in the world for this man. I'll wait for him here until I turn into a mummy.

At eight o'clock I catch sight of him in his invariable green shirt slowly walking straight toward me.

He is not the least bit surprised that I am still waiting for him. We listen to David Lynch on the influence of transcendental meditation on the creative process and on making our wishes come true. Christos leaves after the end of the talk. I give him my phone number.

I head home with the sense of a mission accomplished.

A week later, while I'm trying to convince a rich Englishman, the husband of a friend of mine, to invest in my magazine, Christos calls. I can't believe it. "I can't talk right now, please call back later."

He doesn't call back.

Life is whirling me every which way, I don't even have time to grieve that my angel is gone. I don't have time to hang around the courtyard of the academy.

But Christos is everywhere. Wherever I turn, I see his defiant smile— the whole city is awash in posters with his face. Ads for the international youth film festival in Sofia, which will begin in a week.

I tear down a poster. So I can at least have you at home, since you haven't called me.

One evening I go into a jazz club with a couple of Frenchies. I've interviewed them about their upcoming film project, which will be shot in Bulgaria. Right as the party is in full swing, I see Christos. I see him from behind, but I know it's him. His exquisite, straight back. There is something in his neck, some dignity, virility, and strength that I can't mistake.

I ditch the Frenchies. Christos and I knock back drinks at the bar, dance and outshout the deafening concert. We invent a dance—we press our heads together at one point up on top and each of us rotates around his own axis, without losing contact. The synchronicity between us is astonishing. We don't get dizzy. It's like we were born connected. Christos is easygoing and doesn't hit on me at all. He is simply there beside me—joyous and full of life.

Around midnight I say goodnight and leave. I park my old Ford in front of my place. I kill the motor and sit in silence. What are you doing here—that voice asks. I'm going home to sleep. How can you sleep when you've left back in that jazz club everything you've been waiting for since forever? March your ass straight back there.

Five minutes later I'm back at the club. He is sitting alone on a chair in the yard of the club, his tousled head tossed back, staring at the starry sky.

He smiles at me and pulls up a chair for me, too.

I stand there by him.

Come. Come with me—the voice orders him.

He gets up and comes with me. He doesn't ask where.

I only live a few minutes away from the club. As we pass by the ground floor of the neighboring building, Christos casually mentions, "Oh, so you live here? See there," he points at the lighted window, "I worked there until recently, doing film portraits of famous directors for a TV show. I edited like crazy every night until 5 a.m."

Shiiiiit, all of these months he was here with you. Only a step away.

We walk inside my place and Christ Almighty, Christos sees his face on the wall.

He looks at me, alarmed.

"I like you," I say.

He examines my place with curiosity. He notices the scrolls of Japanese calligraphy on the walls. His mother's son.

I don't remember exactly what we talk about, but we don't shut up. First we drink all my alcohol, then we switch to tea.

I do a complete tea ceremony. I crawl around the floor in a kimono.

Toward morning we're sitting across from each other at a table—Christos with his back to the window, me facing him. We've drunk up everything we could. Our eyes are heavy.

Between us near the wall there is a vase with a sunflower in it. It has opened its head toward the sun rising behind Christos's back. Both the flower and I are looking toward his delicate face.

I close my eyes for a moment. I have nothing more to say. I only know that I want this man.

I send a prayer to God: Please, God, if there is some way to tell him how much I need him, please, please, give me a sign. I sit and wait.

I don't know how much time passes. I sense that something is happening. I open my eyes and meet Christos's pale face, his eyes fixed on the sunflower.

The sunflower is turning.

Barely visibly, the sunflower turns toward me, toward the dark side of the room.

I think to myself, Wait, don't they turn toward the sun, why is this one . . .

We watch it, not daring to breathe.

The sunflower turns around and stops.

From up close, I see the petals and the perfect mathematics of the head.

I look at Christos. He is dumbstruck and serious.

I collapse onto the table. I breathe. All voices in me are silent. I hear

Christos's voice, slightly husky:

"Manda, why don't you go to bed?"

"On one condition—that you hold me."

Christos carries me in his arms to the futon and carefully lays me down. He lies down next to me and hugs me. We fuse.

We wake up at dusk.

I ask him, "Do you have plans?"

"No."

We don't go out for two days.

We place fruit on our bodies, we feed ourselves with it, we lick up the sweet juice, we make love and fall into a deep sleep.

I buy him a toothbrush and slippers and we start living together. When I collapse into my sadnesses, Christos rocks me in his arms like a little child. As if I'm dissolving in the ocean. I have no boundaries.

I have faith.

Christos accepts me as I am. He delights in what I do, helps me and is proud of me. He is much more experienced in love than I am. His kisses taste of water from a mountain stream. He smells of bread. Christos is love.

Rupen comes back from Sicily, where he had been traveling with his father and the latter's new girlfriend—a well-known singer.

Christos is like an older friend to my son. They stay out all night playing video games. The two of us fight for his attention. Things are happy and free at home!

A month later an Italian director, Ermanno Olmi, recognizes in Christos the knight Giovanni de Medici—an Italian national hero—and steals him away from me for six months. We spend a fortune on phone sex. Only my work on the magazine helps me cope with my love's absence. When he finally returns and we head to the seaside, I get an invitation to take part in a massive project: A European Literary Train, 103 writers from the old continent traveling for two months in an attempt to imagine a Unified Europe, to get to know one another, to give literary readings and to write together. I will represent Bulgaria, along with two of my fellow poets. The train will be leaving in a month from Lisbon and will arrive two months later in Berlin, after passing through eleven cities.

I don't want to part with my love for anything in the world. I call to decline the invitation. Christos is surprised.

"You wanted to travel so badly. Are you giving up on your dreams just like that?"

"No, I don't want to anymore. You are my journey."

"I am everywhere with you. I always have been." Christos smiles enigmatically.

I set off.

Siamese Cats in Brocade Jackets

I'm in Lisbon. I arrive a day before the others, after the miraculous feats of bravery I had to pull off in Bulgaria to get here. The hotel is gradually filling up with lots of writers I don't know. We're about to take off on a two-month train trip around Europe in an attempt to start seeing ourselves as united.

I miss the sign-up for the organized tours of the city, which have been booked up by all the Westerners.

From the first instant I know that I've lived here at some time. I know everything. I want to see two things: Fernando Pessoa's café and the ocean.

I stumble across the first immediately. Accidentally. A dark, long café, with heavy mirrors in Baroque frames. I imagine how Pessoa loved sitting in the very back under the clock, eaten up by anxiety. Now in that spot a tiny old man is asleep, pen in hand.

The city is soft, light, perched on seven hills, with little streets, Moorish white houses with green windows and blue doors and lattices, which slice through pale female faces, their gazes fixed on the street outside.

In front of the doors, there are Siamese cats dressed in little yellow jackets edged with brocade, tied up in front of the entrances like dogs.

As a prank, someone has turned all the buildings with their bathrooms inside out. The walls with their cheerful tiles perfectly weather the rain and the tourist's caress—cold, glazed with an Oriental cleanliness that pushes me toward the ocean stretched out in the valley below. It turns out to be the Tagus River.

Pessoa's café is on the peak of one of the seven hills, more modest than the rest. It is sufficiently steep, tormenting one little streetcar, which, once it has finally clambered up, immediately flips its backside into the air and disappears toward downtown. Like all idiot tourists, I take my picture in a poetic pose in front of the bronze Fernando, who has sat down once and for all on his favorite square.

It isn't mine, though. I set out to look for it. At the last moment I hurl myself onto the streetcar and we flip up our backsides on the way down.

God, how it judders along, coming a hair's breadth from the corners of the buildings, constantly sideswiping some dark magenta bushes, while inside I feel like I'm at a wedding—flowers go flying, snug little aunties in black chatter away and dangle their short, fat little feet shod in neat black shoes. They examine the day as if it were a bride, trading impressions. On the Lisbonites' faces, you can discover traces of all the world's cultures—here an Indian peeks out, there an Arab; the Caucasian has imposed itself on the face, yet the body possesses the grace of an African. At one point the streetcar stops. Some car is parked on the tracks. We wait. We check out the groom. A conversation starts up. The group is cheerful.

A weekday. Around 11:30. They're laughing. The driver sits calmly up front. Now and again he, too, adds something to the party in the car. How funny could it be? We've already been sitting here half an hour. Behind us other likewise out-of-breath streetcars have lined up, other cars, too. Outside, policemen pass by. Nobody notices anything out of the ordinary.

At a certain point, a frightened Indian jumps out of a store across the way with a huge beach umbrella in his hand, tosses his new acquisition in the car, and frees up the tracks. Applause bursts out, the aunties are worked up, their eyes are glittering, the ceremony is in full swing. As we set off, one policeman carefully grasps the Indian by the elbow and presents him with a ticket.

The streetcar shakes me off on the highest hill with the fortress precisely on the spot I will return to over the two remaining days, because. Because this turns out to be my hill.

How should a city be explored? Where should you begin? Maps, guidebooks. Yes, that's the way. They prescribe museums. But since I'm already way outside any type of itinerary, I sit down by a green wooden kiosk at the foot of a gigantic cypress, get myself a beer and a sandwich, and turn the delicate stool in the direction of the river above all those pale pink rooftops. The wind in Lisbon is broad and generous like the overflowing river-ocean. Now here in this place, that refrain about *l'insoutenable legerete de l'etre* floats up again, such lightness, and a place for fado opens. Music about sorrow and the unbearable beauty of being. Then Jeremy Irons appears from around the corner. Tall, lean, drawn, with two thin brackets between which lips are stretched, outlined with the thinnest moustache in the world. The singer on my hill. They're working for me in this city, I say to myself, and am all ears, because fado is sung softly.

The next day at the same time. He is singing again. I hold him with my gaze, he's a little pale, he points at his throat, explaining with a gesture that his voice isn't in great shape today.

The next morning I'm sick, too. Everything is plugged up. My head aches. My nose is running. My throat—a wound. Fuck!

Should I just stay in bed today? But I've signed up for an excursion to Cascais—the summer residence of the Portuguese kings. The ocean is there! I set out. On the way, I guzzle whiskey from the poet George Borisov's hip flask and gargle my wound. I endure it. Yet another stone in the garden of masochism.

They thrust us into some museum, where the mayor of the town, amidst formalities, suddenly launches into an apology to Fernando Pessoa, who several times had written letters requesting a position as librarian in one of the local castles. But alas, his requests were denied. Here it is expected that we, sitting amphitheatrically in this municipal hall, will lift a hand and forgive these sins of generations past, but the only thing we lift are our asses, hauling them over to Pessoa's dream castle.

The waves from the rising tide are already lapping at its foundations. We are met by a wealth of crab, white wine, fish pie, salads, and fruit. Gradually the walls of one of the halls disappear, surrounded on all sides by water, and the concert begins. A Chinese woman, a Russian, a Pole, and a Japanese man are playing Tchaikovsky. The ocean is holding down the drone. My God, what a cozy little castle—peacocks call from its inner courtyard!

A Portuguese nobleman built it for the woman he loved. Here, everything is amorous. One of the organizers explains to me, "We were great conquerors, we were very wealthy—but you'll rarely see huge castles. We conquered lands, but the local populations weren't massacred. We simply mixed and the cultures patiently seeped into one another."

Perhaps that's the source of the softness that floats through the air in Lisbon, especially at dusk, when the sky is blue long after the stars have been put in place.

This is my favorite castle. I would submit a request to be librarian here, too. I look at Pessoa's three applications for that job, under glass. Rejected.

In the meantime, the heat has been rising and I look around for a way to slip away and fall into the returning ocean. But since it's not clear exactly what will happen, I want to enlist the others as well. I conspire, they agree, amazingly easily, and we bombard the organizers with our desire to go swimming. The structure strains, but they can't resist us and soon we are strewn across the central beach like a group of Young Communist Pioneers. Most of us minus swimsuits, including me. George gives me his T-shirt. An army of nude Slavs, we bravely hurl ourselves in. Hooray! We're alive! What joy. Water! Icy! It simply takes your breath away. In any case, I'm hardly breathing with this sore throat. But oh, wonder of wonders—it's as if something tears and the barrier that had been separating me from myself falls away. In that instant, the Journey begins. When I get out of the water, I am completely healthy. I snatch the initiative! For the first time, we put a wrinkle in the itinerary.

In the evening, a reading at the Cyber Café in Lisbon and fado. Computers and people jammed into a glassed-in veranda—the regulars, plus the writers. We listen to fado but the stuff on the street is more real. I make an old dream come true—sitting in a bar with people drinking all around, there's music playing and I'm writing. I sit in front of the computer's glowing screen and string together a love mail. I press the keys gently in the dark, because fado is sung softly.

Lisbon is fantastic at night. At night, too, I'm certain—I've lived here at some point. Guarded by a Siamese watch-cat dressed in a tiny turquoise vest. I've dropped love notes through lattice windows to the street singer.

I'll come back, that's what I keep telling myself the next morning as well, as the winds along the Tagus River undress me.

In my hand, I'm clutching a small cardboard ticket with a hole—the ticket for this journey, which begins from Lisbon—a magnificent place for shoving off toward new worlds.

Russian Bath

To move 103 writers through Europe by train. One hundred and three sieves of varying coarseness. The traveler drifts about the world, flaking off the dead cells of the familiar.

Russia

Russia, of course. That soundless centrifuge. I know it had to happen to me. One of the reasons for my being on this train. Petrograd. It is not made of stone, as I imagined it from films watched in my childhood. A city built with a flourish. A frayed, former beauty. A city-façade. A ghost of a drive toward Europe.

The Corridor

Hotel Oktyabr. They gather up our passports. Third floor, room 3835. One hundred years ago they thought horizontally here. This isn't a hotel, but a fortress, running on for miles. I drag my heavy travel bag to the elevator and then set off down the long corridor with rooms lining both sides. Rooms, rooms, rooms. From time to time, islands, mid-corridor landings manned by a fat woman—the vigilant Soviet *dezhurnaya*, keeping an eye out for anything suspicious. I walk past three such stations, run across three *dezhurnaya*—absolutely identical. What shortcut did she dash through so as to always end up in front of me, fused to the heavy desk? After the third station I start suffocating. This corridor has not been aired out in 150 years. They didn't foresee windows. They've walked here in their long overcoats, they've slept, cooked, done who knows what for at least six generations. There's no oxygen.

There's red carpet on the floor. Scanty yellowish light high up above. The air is so thick that I stop, take out a pocket knife and cut a chunk of it.

How do the *dezhurnaya* sit here all day? I breathe with the help of the fans, which cut the concentrate. I can't run with this luggage. I can't turn back, either.

I just want to reach my room.

There are still 400 numbers to go. I try not to breathe. When I inhale the pressed contents of a vacuum cleaner enter me, clogging and scouring simultaneously. Claustrophobia.

In Russia, as soon as we cross the border—where we are stuck for four hours—I sense that time is heavy and moving backward. This corridor is simply never going to end, ever. What's the big deal—it's just some crappy hotel? We watch flophouses in American movies, too. We watch.

But I participated in the experiment called communism.

Suffered its consequences.

As soon as I set foot on Russian soil, every detail speaks to me in a language I thought I had thrust aside forever, yet it turns out that I remember. I have no defenses against Russia. It's too familiar. Too much like the Bulgaria of my youth.

Where is my little piece of beauty?

I can't outsmart this reality. Its enormity sweeps me away.

It is no longer enough to buy myself fruit, to arrange my things.

This I know from my conscious years, from my home: the city is ugly, but it still has some pretty places. I look for them. I arrange my space. I choose which street to walk down. I find pleasant people. I work with them. I discover a mountain and create my own world, then another on the seaside and arrange it so as not to see the henhouses nearby, but only the hill with the wild horses and the horizon. I love a few friends. I read books by people who are long dead or live far away. I play several sports. I have a wonderful masseuse, a good elderly seamstress with whom I think up dresses. I have a son and a beloved—my boys. Over the last few years, my work. Without too many detours.

Now I'm walking down some corridor and falling apart. All of my certainties, assurances, and optimism have disappeared. I lug my eighty-pound vanity, and the further I go, the more I am nothing.

My head is spinning from this kaleidoscopic inversion of values. Here they're again telling me what to do and what not to do. With no choice. They drag me around to some monuments in Kaliningrad, plug my mouth with flowers when talk turns to their problems. They simply turn off the translator's microphone at mention of Chechnya. Poverty, destruction, absurdity, and lies. I feel like I'm caught in a trap.

The fear that I'll take up my place in line with these wretches.

That I've never actually left it.

I walk. The boards beneath the red carpet creak.
You are poor poor poor
You'll put up with it up with it up with it
Nothing can be nothing can be nothing can be done.

If only I could control my breathing for a while, like the yogis.

India is miserably poor, too. Happiness, suffering, and death are all rolling around on the street, but travelers there don't get depressed. There nobody thinks to lie. To somehow mistake these pictures for something else—to imagine, for instance, that this is a system created in the name of man.

Great idea, socialism: a system in which everyone is equal. If this system is aimed at man and his welfare, why does it create ugliness, poverty, and evil? Why does it export work camps, brutalist block apartments, and so much fear?

An idea that eats people.

Now it has snuck into this corridor, to die in peace.

I walk. I make progress through the concentrate. It lets me pass with difficulty, it scrapes my skin, my insides. Every particle of this air has its own physiognomy. I feel like I can make out those faces. The faces of millions of people not fulfilling their needs. Killed for the fact that they exist.

In the name of?

This stench. This musty, clogged corridor blows away all my defenses. I reach my room after a half hour, willing to commit whatever villainy just for a breath of fresh air. I can't unlock the door. My hand is shaking. Finally—air! I'm breathing!

View of the Moscow Train Station. During the three days we inhabit this place, the story with the corridor never changes. I don't get used to it.

I take a shower. I tuck myself into the bed all alone, subscribed to all the guilt trips in the world—that I'm a bad mother, that the people I love will leave me sooner or later, that my thighs are getting more and more hairy and bedraggled, the sagging mouth, the little pot belly. There's nowhere I can hide or take comfort.

I latch onto an image: dinner with friends in a cozy spot.

Europa Restaurant
The Balkan contingent quickly gathers in the cultish architecture of the

striking lobby, and we set out. I am thankful that we're together. Now we'll take shelter in some quiet place. We'll eat dumplings. We'll drink vodka. We'll forget.

We're walking down Nevsky Prospect. We come across two restaurants—as pompous and cold as funeral parlors. We ask passersby, "Do you know of some little restaurant nearby with typical Russian cuisine?" They shrug their shoulders and keep walking, looking puzzled; they think, they can't remember, they don't know, in any case after ten o'clock it's doubtful. The Balkan contingent smirks and leans back to enjoy the show. I dig in my heels, saying, "It doesn't even have to be on this street. Do you know of any place like that in this city?" Someone recalls one that may be near the Petrushevskaya Metro Stop.

We enter the subway. My corridor was a breeze. Here you can't breathe at all, but at least there's a bunch of us. We breathe mentally. Down we go, the escalators carrying us deeper and deeper. We travel. We suffer it hostilely. If only we'd eaten something, a candy bar at least. We surface. I look for Petrushevskaya Street. Nobody's ever heard of it. The Balkan contingent gives me a snide look. Assholes. I don't give up—I start in with the same questions.

They point us toward McDonald's.

"No, no, with Russian food," I insist.

They don't know. We walk. I don't know where. Ah, to be a guide whom no one trusts. Who is also losing faith. Balkan, all too Balkan.

"There it is," I shout. "There it is."

It glows in a dark little alley.

We are the only customers at Europa Restaurant. The European Football Championships blare from a big screen. Tubular furniture, marble, and dark damask, like a European train station. But oh merciful heavens, finally borscht and chilled glasses of vodka. If you peer into them, troikas gallop by.

The next day we visit the Catherine Palace, jostling with Japanese tourists and other foreigners in a frenzy to see a building totally rebuilt after the Second World War and already completely falling apart. On the way back, I buy myself fruit. I don't go to the Hermitage. I wrap myself up. I want to sleep through these Russian days. On the train, Hercuse from Lithuania had warned me: "To understand it, you don't even need to get out of bed—you lie there, read, drink, and fuck. That's what you've got to do everywhere in Russia."

Many of the writers do exactly that. They respond to the telephone offers. The female writers are not offered anything to fuck.

The Slovenians are the most extravagant—they buy crates of champagne and caviar, rent a little boat, hire whores, and take off for the Baltic Sea for these few days.

By evening, I can't take it anymore and run outside.

Church of the Savior on Spilled Blood

Hey, everybodyyyyy, where is everybody? I'll die if I don't find someone. Shaking, I reach the lobby and run into George and the Swiss guy, along with the Macedonian girl. I'm saved. We set off to see the city and its white night. What punishment. Vengeance in the form of eternal wakefulness. We reach the Church of the Savior on Spilled Blood, with its magnificent sultan's turbans slipped on top of the domes. Orthodox bordering on the Orient.

Our enthusiasm for sightseeing wanes and we look for a spot to refuel. It turns out that around here the average Russian doesn't even think of eating any farther away than Mama's stove. Last night I was asking them about restaurants. One dinner would cost them five months' pay.

We are alone again. This time there's a show, too—chicks in boots. Decadence hovers in the air. Things veer toward excess, pitchers of vodka, dumplings, Cossack dances, and other models straight out of the books.

George recites:

> All the cathedrals are closed.
> The squares are empty
> Why do I live when you are gone . . .

We cry at this verse and drown our pangs of guilt in yet more pitchers. If that wasn't bad enough, I hear myself say, "Hey, let's go to a Russian bathhouse."

We go back to the hotel. George flags down some private Volga, murmurs with the driver. Voilà! We are kitted out with both a car and a driver. Vladilen, from Vladimir Iliyich Lenin, a Russian charmer with that strange cutesy handsomeness, an out-of-work designer. The Swiss guy wants to find some old German books. No problem. So what about a plan? I insist on the bathhouse. Just for us, for a couple hours. No problem. Everything's no problem. How's tomorrow at one? I feel amazing. Luxury in spite of all this destruction. We jump at the chance and giddy up. Adventures. Enough of these films and books about Russia. We're in the womb. Let's have fun! We have another drink on our floor with the other writers and say goodnight.

In the morning I am numb with horror. What are we getting ourselves into?

The backyards of Petersburg. That backstage. I've got a piece of that, too—I tore off a chunk of the smell of cat piss, sulfur, shit, and mold. It wasn't any different back in Dostoyevsky's day either. They take us around to criminal arcades, basements, and attics—they show us German books by the ton, to say nothing of French ones. I keep expecting them to cut my throat, to make me play a round of roulette.

I start getting used to the abrupt attacks of fear and euphoria in Russia.

I look at Chinese porcelain, umbrellas, gloves—grand fragments of other eras.

I read the geography of mold on the walls.

The Swiss guy finds a few trophies for a song and we take off for the bathhouse, to wash away the dust of Europe.

Russian Bath

This Russian bath is clean.

Not that I've been in any others. I keenly watch the sturdy, swarthy kid who hands us our sheets, trying to find signs of impending bloody carnage by the pool. I glance at George—completely calm. We buy a few of the soft little birch brooms and enter the sauna. We sit there for a while. It's a little awkward, since we've been interacting fully clothed for so long. We sit there, sweating, silent. George tosses water on the stones. It's unbearably hot.

Leo asks in broken French, "Can't we leave the door open?"

"No, we can't," George says.

The Swiss guy wraps himself up and endures. That Leo is a real pet—what a combination of strength and defenselessness; without his glasses he is blind as a mole. One of his hands is constantly feeling around on the bench to make sure it's still there. How does he see the sheep amidst the Swiss fog? Leo is a shepherd. He spends a couple months a year roaming the Alps' highest slopes. The rest of the time he writes books in Romansh, a disappearing dialect, and teaches philosophy.

George senses our uncertainty and lays down the rules: "Turn your back toward me." He dips the little broom in the cask of water, into which he has also poured beer, and starts working me over. My body is astonished. The little brooms are gentle and wiry. The blows are strong, yet the skin does not suffer. *Oh bliss!* screams the Slav in me. My stiff back rejoices. Let's crush that fear of destruction! Only a nice hard beating can break down these knots. The relief of being punished. The pleasure of beating and being beaten. That way you don't feel the heat. Funny how we all of a sudden acquire bodies. I pound George's tense back, his knotted body, I can't stop watching myself from the outside. I'm watching to make sure my sheet doesn't slip off. I don't want to overdo it with the eroticism. But the heat gradually crushes all thoughts. I dip the broom and lay into him.

Ooh, you bad boy. Bad, bad, bad . . .

I get carried away.

Leo looks on, shocked. Once again, he asks to leave the door open. No. Lie down! We give him a good beating. We hit. No illusions. We're in Russia. The high alpine shepherd endures it. He groans. Through the steam we can see how the flesh gradually remembers.

Leo moans, "My grandmother is a White Russian."

"Aha, now you're going to tell us everything."

We fly out of the sauna and fall into the icy pool. Blood gallops through veins, recognizing the body. We shout, swim, and fly. Open rooms look out onto the pool. In one of them, someone has discreetly left vodkas.

The shocking alternating of heat and cold, again and again for hours.

The ritual has been worked to the bone and now we maul it. We leave the door of the sauna open. Everyone beats everyone. The beatings unclog a verbal torrent: curses alternate with Russian classics and some of George Borisov's refrains:

Chorniy chyelavyek, chorniy chyelavek . . . ("Dark man, dark man")
or
Supradin, Supradin—such fragile silver wings . . . [1]*

---

[1] "Supradin" is a popular brand of vitamins in Bulgaria; this is a parody of a very famous poem *Butterflies, butterflies, such fragile silver wings* by the Bulgarian poet Nikolay Liliev (1885-1960).

At this point we're tossing just beer on the stones. Leaves are flying everywhere, almost none remain on the birch brooms. We've de-leafed three forests. My skin is slippery, from the beer or the birch I can't say. I flop down in one of the rooms and slam the door. I wrap myself in a dry sheet. I have no idea at all where I begin and where I end. It doesn't matter anymore. Now that's how I understand "no borders."

Vladilen is waiting for us at the entrance. He gapes at me open-mouthed. After all those screams, moans, what must he have imagined was going on in there? Well, I won't disappoint him. I wink at him and dash into the changing room. In the mirror I see that all my skin is covered with bruises and cuts. Jesus, how am I going to spin this one?

"They'll be gone in three days," George knowingly reassures me.

Hungry and thirsty, we pounce on our humble guide.

He racks his brains. "I know of one place in the new part of town."

"No! Not in the new part of town," I burst out. No more panel blocks ever again.

We land in some ultra chichi Pushkinesque café—we drink vodka. The more vodka, the more guilt. Vladilen drinks tea and turns down the vodka. He looks at me intently and asks, "What do you write?"

"Poetry."

"Can I read some?"

"Yes."

Then he adds softly: "A little while ago, when you came out of the bath, you had this look in your eyes."

"It's from improved circulation," I mumble.

He feels like talking. I don't have the energy. I don't feel like speaking any languages. The Swiss guy and George go to buy *matryoshka* dolls from Vladilen's wife.

I head back to the hotel for a nap. I'm walking along Nevsky Prospect. Just a half hour and again I'm a knot. The attempt to sneak away via the bath-house has only succeeded in stripping away three more layers of skin. Thus flayed, Nevsky Prospect is also a constricting corridor. Against the backdrop of dirty façades—un-rouged corpses with windows neglected since Gogol's day—I jostle against the wretchedly dressed, dead-tired people with their sad faces. Gaping casings alternate with Armani and Thierry Mugler store fronts. A little cocktail dress for only a schoolteacher's entire annual salary. I want my bed and nothing else. I'm tired. I'll sit down for a bit. I'll rest. But nowhere can you find even an inch where you can stop for a moment. There is nowhere to sit along this street, there are no cafés. Shit, the waterworks again! I'm hungry. I feel like eating sweets. Russia is a constant attack of hunger pangs. I go into a shop. I buy cream and a kilo of pastries. That's how they sell them, only by the kilogram. At the hotel, the ex-Yugoslavs take me in. I devour all the cream, the package of pastries, I dig into their sweet *zakuski* as well. I talk with my mouth full, cursing the system, the city, I get worked up, growl, and with every word sense how the fragile barrier preventing total panic keeps growing thinner; my strength leaves me. They look at me in amazement. *OK, it sucks, but is it really that bad?*

"Look, we didn't have quite that kind of communism." The Macedonian girl tries to restore some sort of balance. "In Bulgaria things were worse."

I thank her for the sympathy. In this city, the vampires of all my traumas and fears have suddenly come creeping out. There's a hell of a lot of us here in this body. Where can I run? Nowhere.

I walk down the corridor. I reach my room asphyxiated and dirtier than ever. I can't fall asleep. I masturbate. It doesn't work. I can't make a phone call. The call won't go through. I can't do anything. On the other side of the door lies the corridor. I run. I lay into it with my heavy treads. I go to the train station. I buy a ten-dollar phone card. I dial Christos' number and as soon as the call goes through, my credit shrinks in half. By the time I say *don't worry, I'm fine,* the card is used up. I buy another one—I get through. On the other end: *What's going on? Why haven't you called for three days? Are you at the end of the world or what?*

This is the shortest fight of my life. I curse and bang down the receiver. This fucking country. This city with its long-since-exterminated aristocracy, with its deserted palaces and all around them a crazed swarm of workers. There's no salvation.. How will I stand another day here? I can't go back down that corridor again. I set out. Since it's so shitty, let's drink it down to the dregs, so here I am again on Nevsky Prospect. The more Russia, the more depression.

Then I remember—the river! Of course. The water, the sun, which won't set until midnight.

White Nights

I suffer the subway, tear off a little chunk of its air as well and here I am at the Neva. I walk down the street skirting the bank. The stream of cars is endless. A five-foot-high stone wall separates me from the river. But there are chinks in it here and there, small quays with steps sinking into the river.

10:30 p.m. The sun has become entangled in the lace of some churches across the way. People are moving past me, all with something to drink and little paper bags of food. I find myself an empty quay.

I sit down, and get up.

Every single sailor in the world has taken a piss here. I keep going. These quays reek; it's enough to make your eyes water. Or they're already taken by heavy women, their primordial busts spilling forth, heads thrown back, they sing and drink. Men are nowhere to be seen. At least not at first glance. In one hand, the women hold a gnawed drumstick, while in the other they have expertly grasped a bottle. If they had a third hand, it would be holding a handkerchief. Women who surely remember the Siege of Leningrad. They have worked in the factories. They've given their lives for the Great Experiment, and now they can barely eke out a living.

Why didn't I think to sit down with them?

Then I hate them. I'm not one of them.

I run on ahead.

As if somewhere up there I'll be able to take back my life.

There is no place for me along the Neva, on the square of the Winter Palace, in this city.

Whores

I'm on my way back to the hotel. I'll make it through that corridor, damn it. I get on the subway. Across from me sits a woman with huge, work-worn feet with long black toenails. She tugs at her wig and looks at me with unseeing eyes. I shut mine and get my bearings from the voice announcing the stops.

At the hotel, several of the writers have gathered on our floor, tossing back vodka and beer. They exchange juicy stories about Russian whores, how they work in pairs, who they robbed and how. We are also furnished with the tragedy of the day, about one who worked on TV by day while supplementing her income by night at the hotel. She has three kids. One of the writers hired her just so they could talk. I can picture them, sitting there writing, while the whores spin tale after tale. Yeah, right.

One passes by. We all turn away.

The Greek guy is in a panic: "I've got the feeling that all women in this city are prostitutes. I just can't tell the difference." A woman in a kerchief passes through the hallway. "Now is that a whore or just a regular woman?"

I don't know. I can't be concerned with his patriarchal guilt trips. Hunger is after me again. I go down to the bar. The clerk is yet another one of the cloned *dezhurnayas*. The sandwiches are lined up naked on plates, black with flies. I ask for tea.

We leave tomorrow. We're free people, right? Everything comes to an end. I whisper to myself: "I am not a prisoner, no, I am not a prisoner in the hotel, in this city, in the country." Maybe I feel this way because everything here reminds me so much of what I don't want to admit—that my own life is in ruins.

"Ooof, don't get started again," the Macedonian cuts me off. "Stop looking for answers. Stop trying to explain it. You take things way too personally."

Along the corridor somewhere near the third station I hear Arman's words: "I've never loved you. I loved the idea of some sort of femininity and as long as you resembled it or managed to correspond to it, I loved you. When you slipped out of the frame of this idea, everything collapsed."

That's the key!

My whole ten-year marriage was one frantic tiptoeing act, hoping to slip into the idea's frame. Whose idea? His. But Arman didn't know exactly what his idea was, either.

Since you erase yourself, since you don't know what you want you keep standing on tiptoes. That's why I'm missing from all the photos from that period. What's caught is a woman with a taut face. A mask, which represents the idea. But what is the face? Tons of pictures. A woman, upholding some model: the Traveler, the Mother, the Wife, the Intellectual. None of them who she really is.

In Russia, I see the millions who have accepted their fate and endure a brutish life, participating in their own degradation, postponing themselves in the name of the Idea, only to have it fail! That really is a tough thing to swallow.

Even the Russian bath is no salvation.

I've inflicted the same thing on myself. I voluntarily transformed myself into an idea that serves someone else's idea.

Better Russian roulette.

At least I can beg chance for mercy.

The next day we get on the train. At 8 am, the boozer from Estonia has already sat down to watered-down shots of cognac. I'm shaking.

"I'm scared," I say.

"Well, go ahead and be scared," the Estonian replies and pours me a full glass of cognac.

Lyubimaya, Lyubimaya . . . Beloved, beloved . . .

The train slowly pulls up to the platform; the photographers' flashes crackle, TV cameras are rolling. I don't know where we are. In Moscow. We've never been this important anywhere. The image-hunters and I study one another through the open windows. At that moment the Icelandic writer Ilnar leans halfway out the window, waving a bottle of beer, and screams at the top of his lungs: "Hello, motherfuckers!" Man, how they film. Afterward, the front-page headline: *Train of Drunks Arrives in Moscow.*

Buses carry the writerly platoon through the Moscow streets. Everywhere, a nondescript, heavily made-up female face sinking in a silver fox-fur collar watches us from gigantic billboards. *Lyubimaya, lyubimaya!* is written beneath her, and in the upper-right-hand corner: Face 2000. The Greek looks at me questioningly. I nod.

Dusk is falling. Another city. The capital. Glitzy. Western. We turn and, hey look, there's Red Square and Hotel Moscow. I breathe more freely because it is tidy. I'm addicted to luxury. I stroll around Red Square and calm down; now here's a place I can spend these three days. I sit down and look toward the sunset, perched on the world's pate. I veer onto a side street lined with shop windows full of amazing shoes, prices start at $500 a pair. Excellent. Workmen are digging all around. I stare and start swaying to some kind of rhythm. Tiny drills, as big as a hand, nod rhythmically around the excavation site. What strange, battered creatures. They seem alive. I can't look away. There is something enchanting in their shape, in their tenacious beaks. I sit down and watch. All of Russia is in these primitive little rattlers, which, in some unfathomable way, work.

Hrrr, hrr, pfoooey, hrrr, hrrr, pfooey, hrrr, hrr . . . pfooooey . . . hrr . . . hrr . . .

Fight Club

In the evening I discover a techno-cinema-gambling-striptease club on the street with the drills. We're drinking beer. In the room next door, they're showing *Fight Club*. Young people are watching, lined up along the walls. I hop over there from time to time, torn between the desire to watch the audience, which is completely absorbed in the film, or the brutal brawl on the screen. Watching *Fight Club* in Moscow! The characters are wading around some flooded house, not far from Tarkovsky's style, except they don't move glasses with a glance. The Stalker here doesn't waste his time spewing out philosophical parables, but gets right down to business. It's an action flick, after all—a huge melée breaks out, explosives get made, everything is going according to plan: the Empire of Money is being destroyed. In *Fight Club*, we're in pre-Zone times. I try to imagine how this film must look to them in Moscow, one of the most criminal cities in the world, where they dole out brutal beatings and toss dismembered bodies in trash bins. Only it's not from boredom. Not because they suffer from insomnia. Not so as to escape from the murderous rhythm of consumption. But rather to enter into it.

How ironic: Brad Pitt and his doppelgänger want to reduce America to the state of Russia, where everyone is equal, because they're poor. And during the breaks, to keep in shape, they beat the shit out of each other. The mesmerized spectators in this techno club would give anything to have their credit cards, tidy homes on the 17th floor of some skyscraper, and everything straight from a catalog, especially without too many philosophical discussions. Even at the price of eternal insomnia.

Talk Show 1

The next morning we're on a talk show at the Union of Journalists. It will be filmed for television; the most famous contemporary Russian authors are taking part. The seats for the audience are already filled with journalists and critics, there is no room for the trainload of guests. The Romanian writer curses and leaves in a huff. We stand. In the hall, vanity of vanities, all is vanity—people are running back and forth, working, but with no visible results. Some particular Russian syndrome. The director of the project, Thomas Wohlfart, signals to me and the female writers from Denmark to sit with him at the table for discussion. We hear some fat lady say to George Borisov, "Those three chicks! What the hell could they tell us, they're far too cute."

They start. The Russian writers in conversation: a closed, self-contained system.

The topic is *The Fate of Literature in the Context of New Means of Communication:* "Humanity won't leave this simple form behind, the word is powerful, the writer is a technicality, writing is just now getting started, the flame has not died out, it'll always crop up somewhere."

Where am I? I wonder. What time is it, or better yet, what year? *The year 2000, my beloved, the year 2000.* We get no chance to speak at all. All around me, they keep going on like coiled springs.

"But the good thing about the Internet is that you can publish without censorship."

"It is easier to love the whole world than a specific person."

"How does women's writing differ from men's writing?"

"Will Europe be forced to unite with us, and not just us with it?"

Talk Show 2

After that, while I'm gawking at some photo exhibit in the lobby, everyone else disappears somewhere. I look for them. No one can give me directions. They don't know. It turns out that they are at the journalists' restaurant. I try to get in, but a beefy man stops me:

"*Where* are you going?"

I show him my badge.

"Impossible," he says. "Everything is already full."

Why do I feel like I've already experienced this? I look at him for a second, tell him to fuck off and go in. George waves at me from one of the tables.

A salon. An official luncheon. A middle-aged guy with a balalaika and slicked-down hair, sitting on a chair amidst the tables, playing quietly. Yet another Russian touch for dummies.

Actually, who gives a shit about Russia's image? A broken record. We're so big and inescapable, inside the corpse.

There's borscht, pickles. "Eat," George tells me, "this is one of the tastiest restaurants in Moscow."

Everyone is terribly busy with the hors d'oeuvres. In Russia, whenever food shows up, people disappear. They're here, but they've entirely transformed into whatever it is they will shortly be swallowing. Want, hunger, wars still linger. They eat silently, urgently, wrapped in a fleeting shame, which they hope to scatter. Shame not so much from the fact that they are hungry, but from the fact that hunger casts doubts on their spirituality.

We're at the same table with Kudamova, the fat lady who argued during the debate that as long as man is unhappy, literature is not endangered. I sit there eating, drinking vodka, and keeping quiet. I simultaneously feel hungry and like throwing up. Still, the hunger wins out. George tries to brighten the atmosphere and introduces me. He explains who Kudamova is, what a great poet she is. She looks at me ironically. I'm one of the cute ones, right? How could I know enough about suffering to write?

"Why are you sad? *Ustalaya?* Tired?"

"*Nyet.*"

"Don't take it so personally," Kudamova smiles condescendingly, exchanging conspiratorial glances with a slug to her right.

His gaze agrees: *I'm one of the cute ones, and the cute ones should always be smiling.*

"Everything here is so sluggish, so slow," I articulate the uppermost layer of my anger, "so pointless and retrograde. Those things were already debated ten years ago."

"You are ill-prepared to make such statements. In order to understand Russia, you need time."

"I don't need any more preparation to sense it. You live like cattle"— I'm picking up speed now—"yet at the same time you claim to inhabit some unbelievable spiritual realms."

"The problem in Russia," Kudamova explains, looking right at me, "is that we cannot make culture coexist with civilization."

Yet another cliché, I say to myself and let it pass.

But she insists: "Did you understand me? We have culture, but it does not produce civilization."

"So why don't you do something?"

"What? Where? The social fact itself is lacking."

I interrupt her: "So that's why everything takes place inside the soul? Are we in Tibet here, or what?"

"Why are we constantly talking about Russia, my dear?"

"Because you haven't asked me anything about Bulgaria."

"If ten people get together and one of them is Russian, all they'll talk about is Russia," the slug pipes up.

"Nothing can be done," Kudamova continues. "You cannot even begin to suspect how much we have changed in only ten years. This is a huge country. Infinite."

"America is huge, too."

"But they have a system."

"Then just do something for yourself every day."

"Like what? Nothing can be done," Kudamova says.

"Then put up with your dictators. It doesn't matter who they are; the difference is minimal. Someone to beat you and to love you—*Batyushka Gosudar,* Big Brother—to take the responsibility, to have someone to hate and heap on all the blame." There was no stopping now. I cursed myself for cutting Russian language class. I didn't have enough words, but I would write on my skin what was welling up inside if I had to. George kept silent, quietly feeding me words when I got stuck: "You want a master, stuffed with the maggots of power, of evil with no corrective, so you can retreat into your souls and drown yourselves in vodka. You speak in quotations alone, believe in miracles, and accept with relief the periodic bloodletting here and there in the empire. In the end, some night you'll piss in the czar's Chinese vases and shoot him along with his family, if he hasn't beaten you to it. No. I don't want any more of this Russia. Its myths are more convenient—the farther away, the better. Dostoevsky, Gogol, the music, Tarkovsky, vodka, and caviar. Yes. I prefer to consume it at home in my slippers. A little suffering Made in Russia, but with a remote control, if possible."

I hear my voice echoing. It has gotten quieter.

George has fixed his eyes on his soup. The fat-ass has calmed down, satisfied. She loves being beaten, this woman. The slug's eye prowls over me, surprisingly directly.

What do I want? I don't realize it then.

I'm furious, furious! I refuse to be the only one getting depressed. I want revenge. What did they take us for with that talk show? Are those really the Russian writers of today? No. Those are the ones allowed to participate.

I grow terrified.

I have no defenses against Russia.

There's no outside. No inside.

Everything is one.

I recall a joke about a guy standing in front of the door of a house, pounding on it and screaming: "Let me gooo! . . . Let me gooo! . . . Let me go out!"

I'm in Sofia. I'm tidying up at home. I'm creating civilization. Civilization!

I toss out the scraps of smells from Petrograd and, by chance, start reading a newspaper by the dumpster: *Incident with a Russian Submarine in the North Sea.* The Russians leave their sailors to drown. Photos of the teary seamen's wives praying.

The world wonders: What is going on?

Borscht

Boil two pounds of beef breast in two quarts of water. Strain the broth and separate the meat from the bone. Sauté five cloves of ground garlic in three tablespoons of olive oil until they release their aroma, then add half a head of celery, two onions, one small beetroot, two carrots, and one bunch of parsley, all chopped into thin sticks about 4 cm long. Reduce the heat and cover the pot. Once the vegetables have softened, add the broth, meat, and several potatoes cut into large chunks. When the vegetables are almost cooked, add two handfuls of finely sliced cabbage and two grated tomatoes. Mince several pieces of bacon with four cloves of garlic, half a bunch of dill, and a bit of parsley. Add the resulting paste to the soup, letting it just come to a boil before removing the borscht from the heat. Serve with a spoonful of cream and shore up with vodka, as much as you can handle.

Photograph

For several days now I've been trying to come up with a photo for the cover of my gender magazine. I see the picture I need at the *New Generation* exhibit at the French Cultural Institute. That's what I need, a picture of a pretty girl with a huge cold sore on her mouth. She's looking into the lens with wide-open blue eyes, while another girl is draped over her shoulder, stroking her face. I find the artist, Ioan Ruslo, a French photographer with Italian blood. When we meet he looks to me more like an Arab, a Jew, a Bedouin, a Bulgarian, like an angel in a devil's disguise, surely that's one reason he can't stay put in France for too long. He is interested in the world's freaks. In a few weeks he has gotten to know Sofia better than I do, its mysteries, its nightclubs, its dark and even darker places. His mother is a follower of the great Bulgarian spiritual master Petar Deunov. He came to Sofia to create a portrait of the young generation. The faces captured do not differ in any way from the young people in Paris, London, or New York. He gives me his photo. Now all I have to do is find the girl and ask for her consent to be on the cover. All we know is that her name is Maria and she's a model. I search for her, with zero luck. A week goes by. Maria becomes more and more mysterious. The designers who have worked with her tell me that she is amazing and really strange. They give me phone numbers, but the voice on the other end invariably replies that Maria has never lived there. They have never heard of her.

One night, around one o'clock, Ioan calls and invites me to some party. We drive for a long time through the outskirts of Sofia, through ever darker and dirtier neighborhoods. People with swarthy skin stop us. They want to get in my car. We wrest ourselves free and finally arrive at some dodgy-looking apartment buildings. I wonder how he can find his way around. I'm shaking. Where am I? There are no lights.

We climb up the dark stairs, ring the bell at some door. It opens up. Music and a single beam of light that blinds me surge from the darkness.

They ask us, "Who the hell are you?"

Paranoia grips me: "I, I'm nobody."

They reply from the darkness: "Nooo, you're not nobody. We know you, and the guy next to you."

Kafkaesque guilt creeps over me.

"What are they saying?" Ioan asks me. The beam strips us.

Suddenly a light flips on inside and there's a burst of laughter. We are in the spotlight of a camera. Behind it stands the girl from the photo, whom I've been looking for all week.

We go in. The floor and the walls have been scratched by the claws of a monster who has been growing there for a long time.

There is nowhere to sit down inside the apartment, which is full of boys dressed as women and girls embracing other girls. They are all piled on top of each other like small, newborn puppies in a cardboard box: warm, pressed together, seeking caresses, biting, whimpering, pissing. In the kitchen, a naked boy is cutting salami with an enormous knife.

I find a chair and freeze on it. I remember that I have a child. I'm afraid. I gradually realize that they are so drunk and high that they are not here at all. I try to communicate. I feel like a walking status quo.

Maria is the most with it. A law student, she also studies psychology. She takes part in fashion performances for fun. I explain why I'm looking for her. I explain to her what *Post Scriptum* is: a magazine that gives space to the female voice and attempts to unearth the forgotten dialogue with men in new social realities. She agrees to be on the cover.

Ioan is in his element, crawling on the floor, he has fused with their world and is snapping away like mad. They pose, coolly distracted. Our narcissism leaves us last.

I'm slightly nauseous from this mauling of my world.

I live in a city I know nothing about.

Osaka

I wake up early. Tired. I lift the curtains slightly and see that Osaka is already racing furiously down its well-worn highways. We are on the top floor of the swankiest hotel in the city as guests of the European cinema festival. Christos is sleeping sweetly. He'll sleep all day if I don't wake him, with his pink muzzle and thick chestnut locks, which I love to dig my fingers into. Things would be completely different if he had woken up already. We would be breakfasting by the waterfalls flowing through the bamboo and orchids, rustling newspapers, hearing the frenetic cries of good morning, bathing in the security of businessmen and their hard-set wives.

How I would love to be able to simply flip over and fall back to sleep in the obliging darkness provided by three thick curtains, snuggled up to Christos and his scent of cookies. But for two years now, someone has been waking up inside me. She wants to get up early. She doesn't care about my exhaustion and imposes all sorts of activities on me, immediately. Thousands of thoughts rush into my head about everything done and not done, who said what yesterday—shards of dreams go flying and I have to leave the bed hastily so as not to go mad. I open my eyes, and if it's a bright sunny day outside, I cover my eyes so as not to see the light, the dawning day and all that impendingness. The horror that yet another day is opening up and I don't know why I'm living it. The question of what to do crashes down heavily, and on top of that, pressing down nice and hard so it can't move, comes the answer that solves nothing: Work, work, and only useful things, investments in surety with nothing for the soul! My life is literal, without play, without celebration, as if the better part of me, bored of waiting for me "to survive," has gone off and rescued itself somewhere. But where? Before, through writing, I somehow seemed to secure distance from myself: it is nice to stand alone. I find myself interesting. I have a sense of something that is about to happen.

But I don't write anymore. The muteness obliterates.

I go into the gold and marble bathroom and stand in front of the mirror. From the side it multiplies me into thousands of profiles. My body is quite a bit younger than my own feeling of myself. Wrapped in silky skin, it's exactly what's needed, accommodating both for dancing as well as for love, and for singing, and for swimming. My breasts are small and shapely. The face before me is that of a sleepy woman of undefined age. We stare at each other for some time.

"I don't know you," I tell her, like in that joke about the guy who woke up, looked at himself in the mirror and said: "I'm not going to shave you, too!" I turn on the water to fill up the bathtub. *I'm not going to brush your teeth. I'm not going to comb your hair. I'm not going to let you out. I'm not going to dress you. I'm not going to caress you. And I'm not going to put lotion on you.* I make terrible faces. She retaliates with Gorgon grimaces from the corners of cathedrals and medieval castles. Then I laugh. Her cheeks prick up, her big teeth show, yet the eyes remain frightened. The woman in the mirror has a terribly fake laugh. That isn't working today. I speak in a nonexistent language. She howls, bugs out her eyes, spews out combinations of sounds. I laugh. *Oh, so was that it? Well, go ahead then.* Water and bubbles crash down into the bathtub. I dilute them with my bubbling words.

"Who are you talking to in the bathroom? Keep it down." I hear Christos's voice from the bedroom. He gets terribly angry when I wake him. I shut the door. The face in the mirror has livened up a bit. I tell her *Fine, I'll bathe you.* We sprawl out in the bath. Warm water is good. Always.

The festival of European cinema in Osaka is taking place in a futuristic complex of glass and metal, built on land wrested away from the sea by encasing tons of trash in concrete and topping it off with a gigantic aquarium, restaurants, movie theaters, and fast-food joints. This place, jutting out into the sea, ends in a harbor where boats from everywhere are constantly arriving and disgorging passengers. I sit there all day, watching the arriving and departing boats. I listen to the flamboyant little voice announcing the timetable. In the East, if you are a woman and don't speak with the intonation of a five-year-old girl, then your chances with men are surely nil. It's like sitting under some socialist-era loudspeaker. I roll around on the benches like a tramp, in my velvet Armani skirt and Fendi boots. The Japanese refrain from gawking at me only out of politeness. No one here stretches out in public places. The sun is miserly and there's no escape from the little voice, which sonorously stabs the space with time-tables. I am uncomfortable; the feeling is sharp. I go to eat. They're singing there, again squeakily. To make up for it I order hot soup with fat shrimp. I'm having a crappy time, because I'm alone while everybody is focused on Christos. Often in these situations when I am not the center of attention, I disappear for myself as well.

Christos played the main character in a film directed by Ermanno Olmi, a Palme d'Or winner at Cannes and one of the dinosaurs of European cinema. For six hours now the Japanese journalists have been torturing him, but there's no getting out of it. He's here to give interviews. Finally the time for the screening rolls around. Whole classes of school kids wait to get in, tickets in hand. They make them sit on the floor.

After the film, they invite Christos on stage and ask him questions about knighthood, as if they don't have their very own samurai. Dobri, who is studying diplomacy in Osaka, is translating for him. But he doesn't seem quite up to snuff this afternoon, since he can't completely catch the questions. Since morning, he's been sucking on a little hip-flask of whiskey, hidden in the inside pocket of his impeccable suit coat. He has mastered the Japanese's own expressionlessness, because the whole time he staunchly remains on stage next to Christos, who starts answering them in English. The amazing thing is that the path to their past passes through Europe. Lost self-confidence and an attempt to recognize themselves.

When it's finished, I'm sitting patiently in the lobby, watching the college students and school kids meekly line up to get autographs from my knight and talking with a fat black woman, who has been assigned to us for these few days as a personal chauffeur. While she drives unconscionably fast through the wild traffic of Osaka, she turns around to make sure she hasn't spilled us out around some curve and shrieks: "Oh my Goood, he's famous! He's famous, and he's in my caaar!"

Her name is Josephine and she's an English professor at several universities in Osaka. Like many of her colleagues, she is volunteering at the festival. I feel uncomfortable that she has to wait around all day in front of the cinema because of us.

"Oh, don't worry, I never wait. I have a book." Josephine pats the book she is reading with her big paw. She is relaxed in her roomy shirt, her black flip-flops on bare feet and her grubby woolen stretch pants. I'd like her to be my aunt, or at least my neighbor, so we could chat over the fence with baskets of fruit at our feet, inviting each other for coffee and doughnuts in the morning.

It's the last day of the festival. The little Frenchie who is organizing it invites us to dinner. We drag ourselves to some cheap chicken restaurant. There are also some other European Union types around the table.

"Let's introduce ourselves and say who's who," the Frenchie suggests. He's already fairly tanked.

In fact, he couldn't care less about having dinner with us, but etiquette calls. They start from the other end of the table. Some Belgian goes first, a psychoanalyst and critic of early twentieth-century European film. Next to me is a young, ambitious Japanese woman who has lived in Paris, Frenchie's girlfriend. We sit and listen to the projects, titles, and other facts from the Belgian's biography; then a German guy starts up, a judge for the Berlin Film Festival. We all nod, smile, and demonstrate interest. The Frenchie once again sings his song, which we've been hearing at cocktails and festival meetings for several days now, about how hard it was to put together this festival, how there's no cash, how the Japanese don't give money for culture. It's the typical European intellectual's sniveling for money; that word is heard at least once every five seconds. The Japanese woman introduces herself as a visual artist and as Frenchie's right hand, trying to help out with the festival from Tokyo. My turn comes. I feel sick. I know that if I list off everything I do, it won't sound serious. How would this sound? "Editor-in-chief of a magazine about female spirituality and integration between the sexes, which doesn't come out anymore. I have my own center for psychotherapy and meditation called *The Yellow House,* and after work I pay tons of money to recuperate. I host a show on Radio France International about psychoanalytical and gender readings of contemporary art, and in my free time so I can shut up for at least a short while, I listen to the mountains and put out discs of nature sounds. I have three books of poetry; I write a little prose, too, but for ten years now my pen has gone dry. In general, I've dried up quite a bit, otherwise I love sports and am the mother of an eighteen-year-old son. I'm forty-six. I live with Christos, who is sixteen years younger than I am. He is so beautiful, sexy and famous that sometimes I get terribly scared that I'll lose him. Lately I've been doing performances and installations. I don't feel particularly attached to any of these roles."

I mentally chew over this pretentious statement. Can I explain the juggling act of a woman who had the nerve to work with culture in a country transitioning to capitalism, which has no particular need for art? Maybe it would be better to say: "I hate CVs, because they cramp my style. I am so afraid of life that I'm not totally in anything. I am the most nihilistic toward myself and I don't have the self-confidence to define myself. I see even less point in doing so after the representative samples I have just heard." But instead, I say: "Look, I, I." Everyone at the table is staring at me. "I'm having an identity crisis."

I sense horror swelling up around me for letting slip something too personal. "Would it be acceptable if I introduce myself only with my name? My name is Manda and I'm here with Christos, my boyfriend."

"Just let me add," I hear Christos's voice, "she writes fantastic . . ."

"Christos, thank you!" I kill him with a glance.

He rallies. He takes a breath and says, "OK. I am Christos Zisis—I'm an actor and director. As you already know, I was invited to the festival because I played the main character in *The Art of Arms.* And, of course, I am here with my darling Manda."

"I'm their driver!" Josephine quickly spits out.

"I'm their translator," Dobri quickly finishes off the introductions with an absolutely indifferent face.

Silence sets in. We hear shouts from the kitchen. It feels as if the end of the table, where the projects are sitting, suddenly flips upright like the nose of the sinking *Titanic,* while we bottom out somewhere amidst the depths of the blue haze. Then something suddenly judders, bubbles gurgle, and we again find ourselves in the light of the restaurant, barely able to take a breath, huge mouths split wide open with laughter amidst the pale perplexed faces of the Euro snobs.

Until the end of the evening, our part of the table has fun examining the national character of the Japanese, the Europeans, and the Americans, while at the other end attempts are made to hash over festival realities. Josephine has succeeded in coming to hate the Japanese, most likely due to nostalgia for California. She cusses them out good and hard, calling them vampires, because they manage to suck everything out of you from behind their impenetrable Eastern masks, without giving anything in exchange. That's why she has thought up her own system for deciphering Japan. She goes to cooking classes and lessons in classical Japanese dance. I try to imagine her in a kimono.

Our noisy mood overflows into a merry tour of "Osaka by night," in what has become our typical arrangement these days: Dobri next to Josephine in the front seat and Christos and I in the back. She drives as fast as ever, hollering things about the places we pass. We whiz through the neighborhoods with private clubs, by some replica of the Statue of Liberty, and the oh-so-hip crowds, high and drunk Japanese kids in expensive American convertibles. In the end, we get lost in an attempt to find our translator's dorm. Around 4 a.m. we leave him in his bed, together with his bottomless flask of whiskey.

Journey in the Garden

6:30 a.m. Outside, the hill sprawls before the veranda, only its peaks licked by the sun. Again that same sense of not knowing. Somewhere inside me, Nikula, who has surely got up before five, is crocheting a pillow and grumbling: *You should have been out running a long time ago. Instead of washing up, getting neatly dressed and starting to write while you're still fresh, you dawdle around,* my mother adds, *and just look at your hair—a woman can't go out looking like that.* In the morning you're angry at yourself, in the afternoon at the whole world.

Damn, it's packed here today.

I warm up a little tea, put on my torn overalls, and pull on a thick sweater.

A scruffy person within me rebels: "I'm gonna sit here until I figure out what I feel like doing."

I sit down under the quince tree.

I watch the sun reacquaint itself with the hill.

I watch the awakening of the birds, the swaying of the willows in the valley below. Just like that, until time melts away and I no longer know who is watching all that. I need to bow. My whole body strains upward in prayer and then returns to the ground. I stretch upward and shrink down. I slowly return to my day. I put on twenty minutes of silence. I sit down, until I hear the three gongs. I open my eyes. The world is there. More brilliant and enormous than I remember it.

I set off toward the river, on a hunt for pumpkin blossoms amidst the potato fields. Bees sleep in these earthy bullhorns. I carefully nudge the flowers to drive them out.

At home, Christos has also left the bedroom. I put on a killer techno track. We jump around on the veranda. I like the softness of his movements.

My love is cheerful and light. I love this Greek man. His neck smells of caramel. I don't want to part with these aromas. Besides the usual herbs, I put a stick of cinnamon, several cloves, and apple slices in the boiling teapot. Swathed in scents, I, along with my teapot, enter the dark gas chamber with the computer. As I write, some movement draws my attention: a big forest ant is climbing up the dome of the window. It reaches the middle of the arc and falls. I try to understand it. It crawls over the dome with its back to the ground, manages to hang on, studies it with alarmed antennae stretched out ahead and crashes down (what a verb for an ant!), and then starts climbing up again. Every time the ant goes flying down, something heaves in my stomach. The ant keeps at it almost until lunchtime.

Outside Christos is wrestling with the yard. He has declared war on the creepers in the ruins there, armed with a scythe, a hoe, scissors, and a rake. His cheerful songs can be heard as I cook.

Pumpkin Blossoms Stuffed with Rice

Over a slow fire, heat a clove of garlic, a pinch of curry, a knife-tip of cinnamon, a pinch of nutmeg, a ground clove, and a pinch of white pepper in four or five tablespoons of olive oil. Once the spices release their aromas, add a cup of rice, stirring until the oil and aroma have been absorbed. Pour in a cup of hot water so the mix bubbles up a bit. Fill the blossoms with rice, twisting the ends like little bundles. Grease an earthenware pan with olive oil and arrange the filled pumpkin blossoms on it. Pour another cup and a half of hot water over the dish and bake in the oven, first at high, then at medium heat.

The blossoms can also be filled with four cheeses—Roquefort, feta, smoked cheese, and parmesan; again bake in the oven.

But if you need hors d'oeuvres for beer, make a mixture thick as porridge from one tablespoon of flour, black pepper and beer, dip the blossoms in it and fry them lightly on both sides in a little olive oil until they turn pinkish.

We eat lunch.

"How happy and calm I am here. It's amazing living in this rhythm," Christos confides. "In the city, the profit-driven model that's forced on me repulses me with its aggression and ambition, while the idiocy on the streets gets into me without me even seeing it."

"You'll find your own model," I say. "It depends on what you're ready to give."

Pleasure, pleasure, look for it in what you do. Only that is close to the center. The bells on the veranda softly jangle.

"Come lie on my shoulder," Christos says philosophically.

Blissful, we sleep beneath the swaying canopy of the big bed on the veranda.

At dusk, stiff from sitting in front of the computer, I do a chakra breathing meditation. I love this meditation. It is three fifteen-minute cycles of breathing through each of the seven chakras in turn. Toward the end of the last cycle I sense my body as a straight and clean tube through which energy freely descends and ascends. During the quiet phase I slip under the canopy, so as to escape the gnats, and lean into the crickets' drone. Right in the throat, where the chakra for expression is, the desire to sing appears. I'm making a really cool CD with quiet songs. I see myself dancing. I have so many movements inside me. Afterward these thoughts, too, sink amidst the crickets. The body disappears and I am simply there, hanging in the warm dusk above the bed, when the gong startles me. I'm monstrously hungry.

After dinner we take a thick goat-hair blanket, a couple pillows, and a bottle of wine. We go to the ruin in the yard, of which only three walls remain. Between them, Christos has lit a huge fire from dried grass, elder cut from the garden, and two fat, rotting stumps that have been wallowing by the gate for years. The moon is filling out, staying with us a little longer each evening.

"Now here's a journey in your very own yard," Christos boasts. "Now we'll experience the energy of this place."

The fire swallows up the hay.

"When I look at it, I tense up," I say.

"You're crazy."

"I'm gluttonous, Christos. Inside me there's a scared and insatiable idiot who never sees what's been done, but constantly looks ahead toward what is coming. What if I'm always stuck in the foothills, constantly asking for more? I'm afraid of whether I can hack it, of whether I'll achieve something. This game is never going to end. I can't simply watch the sunset. I won't ever be able to feel joy again."

"Until your desires cease," Christos smiles faintly.

"Before I could marvel for hours at the things around me. But for years I've been struggling, accomplishing, proving myself, without a whit of happiness. Without a break. What if I drop dead in my tracks?"

"You didn't know as much before. Now the sunset isn't just a sunset. That's why you're anxious. But if you still have things to give yourself, then give them." Christos makes a broad gesture with his cigarette. "How long have you been wanting to write your book? You've always known what to do. The problem is that you don't believe in yourself."

"It's true, I just follow my routine. But it doesn't lead me to myself. I want the celebration and the spontaneity back. The simplicity. They got lost somewhere along the way."

The crickets thunder in our ears. Christos hugs me and says, "They'll come back. They're here. Just look."

Wind bursts through the door of the ruins, fanning the fire. We lie there, pressed against each other between the stone walls upon which strange shadows are now creeping, while the black sky hangs above us, strewn with stars.

"Christos, it's so lovely for our houses not to have roofs."

Mask

A crystalline morning after yesterday's rain. I run three kilometers to the bridge. There, a thin finger of fog springs from the ravine, playing with the sun and the trees. I stop and close my eyes. My blood rocks my body, my breathing gradually quiets and the babbling of the stream cuts through. I look toward the mountains in Greece, half-submerged in fog. What kinds of places must exist there? I sit down on a sun-warmed curve and shut my eyes. My borders gradually wash away, and I am the awakening birds and river. I see my life very clearly as a garden, from which sprouts all that I dare to sow. Just as I want it to be.

When I get back, the house is fragrant.

Christos is making coffee, slightly rumpled from sleep. I envy how when he gets up in the morning, Christos is slow.

"I'm crazy about the smell of coffee." He dreamily sniffs the air and takes out a cigarette.

"I'm no longer crazy about anything."

"Except me," Christos laughs and gets ready to dye my hair, putting an apron on over his bare chest. I apply a mask of clay. My face gradually whitens. Only the eyes remain. On top the dyed hair sticks up like branches struck by lightning. I raise my arms, fingers stretched wide, and slowly lurch toward Christos.

"You're repulsive," he screams.

I am overwhelmed by a fit of idiocy. I make all sorts of faces. Christos takes pictures. I don't care about the camera at all; I look at him obnoxiously, changing states. I cry, I'm frightening, I laugh terrifyingly, then sweetly and slyly. Between the face and the clay a space has opened up for silliness.

We go out to read in the sun with the mask. Christos is amazed by the change. Usually when he is photographing me his attempts to tease out naturalness fail. What freedom the mask gives!

When I was little, my father would take me out on walks on Vitosha Mountain to take pictures of us. My childhood memory of my father is of a man who photographed me. He wanted me to look at the camera, smiling. Sometimes he would fix my hair. This was the only touch he allowed himself.

When I accidentally catch sight of myself in the mirror, my face is sad. The appearance of a camera is a signal to obligatorily ascend to the necessary face, worthy of a picture. Behind the lenses that look at me is my father. Always.

In the afternoon, as I sleep in the big bed on the veranda, I dream that I am in a castle—I put on red ribbons and a velvet tiara so my hair doesn't get messy as I'm out riding. A man is standing and watching me. He likes me. When my hair is ready, I get up, go over to him and kiss him. His lips are cold. The taste of the kiss of a man who likes me. Our gazes penetrate deeply. I jump onto the horse.

I wake up with a feeling of tenderness for myself. I deserve to be loved, and to love myself. The sun is setting. A huge cloud has stopped by the house, ecru with pink.

The next morning, I don't get up to run, to do tai chi, I don't eat fruit with oatmeal. With patient caresses, I wake up Christos. We make love slowly. Our bodies meet and flow into each other. Satisfaction spills out everywhere, its round snout persistently pushing its way out of the most unexpected places.

Diary

Everything in the world exists in order to end up in a book.
Stephane Mallarmé

•

How exhausting it is to walk the path from life to its meaning and back every day. It is high time to pick the green beans from the garden; the flowers need a couple buckets of manure. I need to make little signs with the names of the flowers in the garden on them, so my father or some other enthusiast will not weed them out. The sage in particular, which I have raised from seedlings, looks as homely as a weed, but I don't want to lose even a second of my writing time.

From the window in the bathroom as I shower, I revel in the chrysanthemums in the neighbor's yard below. I watch how his tiny wife pinches off the dry leaves, how she pokes her face in the enormous pale-pink flowers, and I imagine their aroma in autumn. Instead of imagining them hung in that house, I can visit her thousands of times, chat on the steps of the gazebo, touch the chrysanthemums.

I resist going into the room with the computer and afterward again resist going outside the house. I separate writing from life. Getting tied down with one prohibits the other. How to combine them? I stand in the middle, driven from everywhere.

Later, the answer appears: by watching. By constantly tuning into the process of writing and the most ordinary things: cleaning the toilet, spreading manure, chatting with the neighbor. Because everything is one.

I go to get manure, then I'll whittle stakes for the garden and cook.

Chinese Green Beans

In a pressure cooker, lightly sauté four cloves of crushed garlic, several small, dried hot peperoncini, and

ginger powder in three or four tablespoons of olive oil.
When they release their aroma, add green beans snapped
in half and a bit of salt and stir vigorously, until the
greenness intensifies. Add four tablespoons of water and
cover with a lid. First, boil them on a high heat for
several minutes, then for five more minutes over a low
heat. Serve as a main course or as a side dish.

•

I'm writing this in Kovachevitsa. I lift my gaze to the landscape that unfurls itself from the last stony terrace in front of the house. The colors along the ribs of the hill in front of me and the trees swaying in the wind—they can never be written. There an apple tree, there a walnut, there a sycamore, there a willow in the valley—they simply tremble in different keys of green.

•

I lie in front of the fire. After describing the consequences of releasing those snakes and crickets in the basement of the my grandparents' home and being beaten with nettles, an enormous burden has dropped from me. What relief! To be beaten or to write about it? I don't know. As I write, I laugh and cry. I wash wounds.

It's quiet. Christos is sleeping inside. The fire is responsible for me.

For the first time, I truly see the stars.

They stand, distributed between the pillars of the veranda: frames for identical, dark-blue pictures. Only one can contain the moon. In the hours that slip by, it bursts into yet another story and rearranges the space. The frames obligingly offer up their constellations, while some disappear upward into a different, larger frame.

I watch this heavenly show. I feel good. I drift off. I dream of the street that leads to the bakery, but the houses along it are gone. In their place, deep pits dug out by backhoes. They'll be built up. I buy herbs and vegetables from some grannies in front of the bakery, and since Christos has an ache, they advise me to take a cat and put it on the sore spot. I wake up. The fire has gone out. Next to me a cat is washing its muzzle. I tuck it inside my bosom. Soon ferocious purring comes from under the fleecy throw.

•

Every day, the story of my childhood progresses. There is magic in being constant. There is freedom inside repetition.

•

I write in order to stop talking about that which I know. As someone said: "Do not repeat yourself and nothing will be taken from you." The one who tells stories does it so she will be heard. She gives her all so as to stand in the ray of someone's attention. Every story is a piece of her. It is difficult to gather together all those pieces without an audience.

•

My books are my gardens. The stories in them are flowers. I look after them devotedly.

Why should I do it?

So as to tuck them away in a safe place and to open up space for the new to happen.

•

Unlike poetry, prose requires patience, time, and opening up. The text about childhood begins to stray into stories about my present life as well. As I write, I myself change.

All of this resembles trying to listen to several symphonies simultaneously.

•

Living in the city interrupts the periods of writing in the mountains. It tries to wash away the text and stitch me to itself. I wonder how to sustain my motivation to keep writing when I don't know what to write, nor do I remember why I even started this book at all.

•

I found the answer to the question above. As always, a messenger appeared. A photographer, who over the course of a year had been going to school with high school seniors to create an exhibit of photographs and texts about the first generation to grow up under democracy, told me that she sustained her long-term projects by working in parallel on other, smaller ones that keep her awake.

I try to apply this principle to keep myself in shape: I write articles, conversations between myself and space, commissioned by a design magazine. I start making my next ambient CD, *The House of Medusa*, from the cistern in Istanbul.

●

Writing has a point if you say something, if you tell some story, an extraordinary one, if possible. But in the usual course of things, life is not extraordinary. It simply flows by like a river, sometimes fast, sometimes slow, sometimes reaching some bottleneck that it passes through with a roar, rushing through some rapids. What is the important part? The river is important. What about the banks? They are important, too. And the rocks, the bed? They are as well. So that's how I'll write. About all of that. I'll learn to see things-as-it-is and accept things-as-it-is.[2]

The Way as it is.

●

My mother read the first part of the text about my childhood. She said it was a nightmare. The figure of the grandmother is monstrous and there was no love in the whole piece, no velvet. *That's how it was* I tell her. *No, no, who will read such a sad book,* she insists. She prefers glimmers of suffering. The Medusa in the spoon. She wants to read entertaining, topical tales. Things that have sprouted up over the wounds, without necessarily putting them on display.

●

Christos will leave for a month to shoot a film. He's angry that they haven't told him the exact day. For several days, I live alongside him, isolated by the armor and barricades. I gradually go inside myself. In the evening, as he cooks dinner, I stand behind him, grasping his shirt. He turns around. He hugs me and says: *You're so small! I love you!* I don't let

---

[2] See Shinryu Suzuki, *The Crooked Cucumber*. "Suzuki often used a singular verb with a plural subject on purpose" (47) to avoid dualism.

go of his shirt, watching what he's cooking over his shoulder.

•

Having painfully stopped writing.

I know this. I know these accusations every day. The lack of mercy toward myself. I realize that when I approach some painful subject, I need time to get used to the fact that I will speak. That I have spoken about it. I need time to learn the language that has just sprung from this touch.

I'm anxious—the indescribable is enormous.

•

Writing is a wall with glimmers of sunlight. Writing is a fellow traveler. A way to stop. To be open and to accept. To get centered. It is the final refuge. Writing exhausts the shadow. I can share it with others. I talk with my innermost self. It expresses me most fully. I understand things I don't know.

•

I am afraid of life. Writing helps me bear it. I open up space. I pour out onto the pages, so as to free up a place. As I write, I forget living, I watch it from the outside, giving the slowest part of myself a chance to catch up with me. Some people call it the soul.

One thing is certain—once I forget time, that means I'm inside, the indescribable has surrendered.

Writing—a duty with which I ransom myself.

•

I dream of a house made of wood, wattle, and mud, which juts up over the sea on one leg. The waves crash into it; it gives way, heaving from the beating. Any second now it will snap free and sail off. I stand and helplessly watch it trembling above the elements. I want to save it, but I can't.

•

I dream of a house: wooden, one story. The front part facing northeast lets in the cold, which seeps into my bones. I am the house and the inhabitant at the same time. Distributed, constant cold.

I need to sew up the front of this house, like the prow of a ship that cleaves ice. All night I tear off old edging and pile up materials.

Patching up the vehicle.

•

I turn onto a side street on the way to my office and see a man wearing slippers, naked to the waist. He is holding a long stick, thrashing a tree. Heavy yellow quinces are falling. He laughs, talking to someone who can't be seen. He is sexy, homey as he is on that little street with old houses by the park, in the middle of the hot city.

•

Without intending to, the wild geese
leave a reflection
The water unwittingly absorbs their image[3]

---

[3] From a Zen poem.

Nobody

I dream that I'm traveling to a seminar in Varna with my colleagues from the psychotherapy school. I leave my bag with everyone else's luggage and head off somewhere. When I get back, the bus is leaving and I quickly hop on. No one can tell me whether my bag has been loaded. There is nothing particularly valuable in my bag, except my diaries. I suddenly realize that my diaries are my life and if they get lost, I'll disappear. The word-crammed notebooks, those glimmers of my experiences, are the only things I possess.

The driver doesn't want to stop to check. I ask if anyone put my bag on the bus, but my colleagues shrug. They look at me. I don't feel like asking anymore. I feel uncomfortable showing my desire to find my bag. I don't want to be the have-not. Both "not having" and "wanting" accuse me of something shameful. They mark me as "suitable for tossing away." Not having and wanting. I am ashamed of my desires, of the life inside me, of myself. I'm afraid they'll see how big the appetite is. *There it is,* I think in my dream, *no matter what I do, no matter what I present myself as, I'm still terribly vulnerable. I can't ask to stop and look for my bag, because then they'll see. All of it.* I want to scream—*my bag, my life is inside that bag, it's important to me, I am important, let's look for it, please!*—I want to, but I keep silent.

And as always happens in dreams, there is no escape; I'm stuck in this situation for all eternity. Without self-confidence. A NOBODY.

I wake up and realize that in my dreams, I remain that which I am, despite my attempts to grow up.

The nightmare returns.

PMS

I've plunged deep into PMS. I've got heartburn. I eat chicken drumsticks. I watch the Hallmark channel. I'm bawling and find it hard to swallow the fact that I'm eating alone, watching dramas and bawling. I hate myself. And when I'm filled with hate I get uglier and look at least thirty years older. There's not a single tiny place on me or in the world around me that I like.

Six days loom in front of me on the calendar, marked in red. On these days I eat a lot: red soups, meat, chocolate. A deathly chill seizes me, I'm tired, and I don't feel like giving anything to anyone. I just have a huge need for attention. I watch my loved ones with paranoia, especially if they don't play their roles: loving me, cuddling me, being sweet. Oh, how I hate them if they have their own work to do. I want to torture them for years for it, to take away their most precious things, to poison them in small doses and watch them turn green. On these days the princess is a scabby, vicious frog. There's no prince around who would love her when she's that green. No one's love is that deep. All of a sudden—and perhaps all the time?—the prince at hand is selfish, scared. I, too, get scared looking at myself; such a spiteful shadow, embittered, abandoned, needy, and offering nothing except her cruel suffering. No one can keep you company during this suspense. You can only imagine it on the roof of some icy *Runaway Train* (see the film), a fugitive between Russia and America, diverted to a dead-end line.

What I'm trying to say is: *I'm now leaving for Dominica and when I get back your stuff better be gone.* I even curse him—*I hope everything goes well for you, that you thrive, so that you get on with your own life and I don't see you anymore.* During these times I am so easily wounded that I constantly chase my beloved away. I know it. The next month I've already forgotten and by the time I realize it I've already chased him away again. But I don't take drugs. I don't relax. I don't anesthetize myself. I sense life, accept its ugliness straight up. Especially during those six days of the month.

There are some rose-colored glasses of serotonin, some mess of chemicals that slightly disguises the taste of hell. But stringing myself out my whole life just because of these six days a month?

Something in my throat is choking me. I go to unclog myself at the mineral baths.

Today, Monday, it's just me, an elderly lady and a few perky Roma women.

I hate Sundays, so I've come up with not working on Mondays, like the tail end of Sunday, like an expansion, a wriggling out of the pressure of EVERYTHINGSTARTSTOMORROW. What starts? Everyone pushes and shoves on that day, mutually canceling each other out. So Monday turns out to be like a second Sunday, while Tuesday comes like a double-crossed Monday. That's why you can't expect anything to happen then.

On just such a missing Monday I enter the mineral bath in the village of Pancherevo. Generous tits and asses wander through the steam. The water gurgles. I will remember how to live freely. I will learn. Without pangs of conscience: *Do I really deserve it? Shouldn't I be dragging the burden along with everyone else in town?*

Outside the lake has frozen solid. Some fishermen, kids, and puppies are puttering around. Bruegel. Inside the clean pools are steaming.

The water is good.

I sit by a basin in the corner. I'm using a scraper. Cleaning. Bits of old skin fall to the floor with a clatter. I look around to check if anyone can see through the steam. But who cares? At the baths everyone sinks into herself. That's why we're here. At some point the smiling elderly woman crops up next to me and says: "If you're alone, why don't we scrub each other's backs, if you want to."

How could I not want to? I've only got one spot left on my back, surely the dirtiest place of all. I look at her thankfully and soon I am squeezing fat black spots on her back. I can't leave them like that. I squeeze and squeeze. I force out whole horns. The woman is relieved and not in the least embarrassed. I scrub. After a while she scrapes me and even adds afterward, "Your back is nice and red—just like after a good massage." It's something like an apology for this bathhouse intimacy. We've become strangers again.

In Japan in the evening, where they don't even touch for "hello," first fathers and sons soak together, then mothers and daughters in wooden

134

tubs. They scrub each other, touch each other, and chat naked. What've you got to hide when you're naked?

Travelers during the seventeenth century describe how in these parts women would spend whole days at mineral baths with carpets, food, and servants. Ladies would choose wives for their sons there. Naked like that, rumors were really rumors. Small talk makes the world go round. But now they're going to make a ceremonial hall and museum out of the Sofia mineral baths. Good thing I gave a final little performance in the pool—five men on five women, so they made me out to be a proponent of group sex. Idiots! Whatever. Monday.

I soap myself up with rose soap. I scrub myself with a silk brush. While I'm wet I smear myself with two drops of patchouli in baby oil. Rituals! I come up with a special massage—with my knees I rub my eyes and forehead, my whole face. I must look like a cat washing itself. The steam has thickly enveloped me. My skin is smooth, perfectly tailored, beautiful to the touch. Every place on me speaks to me. I'm ostensibly with others, yet I am separate, my favorite thing. Like in the library where we're all reading together, but different books.

Things brighten up a bit. I wonder if I couldn't arrange to spend a few hours at this bath next month when PMS seizes me, because I fall into a stupor and can't even leave the house. The time should be used somehow. To satiate the maw. I'm conscious. Awake, in a way. I'm ready to fight this extreme lack of I-don't-even-know-what substances.

I'll invite my nieces over and we'll have fun spazzing out. To remember the joy before someone shit on me, before womanhood weighed on me.

I could also clear up those days and sink into meditation: not looking anyone in the eye, not speaking for six days. Just following how the breath goes in and out of me.

Or else I could go and blow those days on sex.

But in this condition I'm not much for being around people. Otherwise I really am in the mood for sex. In fact, when they reject me because I've started to prickle, then I really fall heavily into PMS. Sex!!! Once again we arrive at the question of the Other. This is more difficult to arrange. He has to be willing, too. To spend six days in bed on command? OK, maybe not exactly six. In general, once it depends on the Other, everything gets messed up. Because he exists, he's supposedly here, but he's not.

Maybe I could get by with regular masturbation in combination with the other elements of the program. It would be easier to organize. But in the presence of the object of desire, especially in the face of lack of attention on his part, it immediately starts to look like abandonment and I again plunge headlong into depression. Fuck!

The problem is somehow connected to the love object. To my feeling of extraneousness. Not you. Not you. NO! My mother must have threatened me when I was a fetus with thoughts of abortion. And as I create my latest egg, I sink into mourning, as if curetting myself. Every month I hate the body that bloats up eggs and then tosses them out. I don't want to let go, to part with, to force things out of me. During these days I hate with the hate of one forced to give birth. Goddamn it, that's the way I feel every time I get pregnant. There hasn't been a single time when I've been happy about it. Only horror. At some invasion inside me. Pregnancy— always unwanted by the "father," too! How many years will I relive my mother's horror at being pregnant? My rebellion against femininity?

No, this has to end. I will take it on myself!

I watch them, the happy elderly women entering the bath, chattering about something, and I envy them for their freedom, for the future which might contain their bodies. But come on, can they really be that cheerful?

On my way home I stop by the Mr. Bricolage home improvement store.

I buy light bulbs to replace the burned-out ones. Rings for the curtain rods. I realize the futility of this building up in the face of destruction. Garlic and a cross against the dark power. A halogen bulb and a long one-legged lamp for the kitchen to shine in the direction of the dark gaping door.

So here I am: I'm wondering whether to buy a bucket-shaped vase or a barrel-shaped flowerpot. I try out a chaise longue. But I don't give two shits, you see, whether there's a chaise longue on my balcony at the moment or a light bulb above my fucking sink. I'm so sick of scribbling out lists and knowing that when I fix something, something else will immediately break. That's exactly what happens when I get home—I change the light bulb above the sink and the one above the vent burns out. I go to leave and start to give a chicken drumstick to the dog in the yard, and the burned-out light bulb slides out of the trash bag and smashes right in his snout. This kills his appetite and he takes off. I had already broken a dish that morning.

Ash Rose

I'm walking down the street, dressed to kill in an ash rose bodysuit with lace shoulder straps, low-rider jeans, and Mary Poppins-style boots with sturdy heels, which grasp the ankle firmly. I feel light and determined. I breeze past the florist, the greengrocer, the bakery and jump into a cab to go to the hairdresser's. From there I'll go to the radio station for my show, and after that to the Buena Vista Social Club concert. I've got to look good. The cab driver is a toothless geezer. He turns around and while I explain to him where we're going, he stares at me and says: "Wow, just look at those breasts. Beg your pardon, but can I look at 'em just for a minute? After that I'll turn around and keep my eyes on the road."

"No problem," I tell him, "take a look, but then step on it, because I'm running really late."

He smacks his lips, sighs deeply, turns around, and takes off. At a stoplight, he steals another look.

"Ooh, now those are some tits, I tell you!" His eyes are glazed over, his toothless mouth restless, as if any second now he'll pounce on me and start suckling.

"Come on, it's you, it's green." I think to myself: what a tramp I am. A true lady would say, "What do you think you're doing?" and would slam the door, but in me, nothing feels angered.

"I really do beg your pardon! When I was young I was so meek," the old man goes on as he drives, "but now in my old age, I don't know what's gotten into me."

"Better late than . . ." I say, and he deftly finishes off: "There's one dame in circulation, she's gotta be over sixty, but you wouldn't believe the head she gives." And his mouth suckles again.

In front of the hair salon, he gives me one last hungry look, muttering to himself in resigned ecstasy *What a rack, Good Lord, look at those,* and melts into the traffic.

A half-hour later, now with a new hairdo, my hairdresser and I, both wearing ash rose, head for the radio station to do a show about the role

137

of the mirror in her profession. We walk down the streets, hair streaming, and the men look at us. She gives me lessons in femininity. Five hours later, in the packed auditorium, exhausted from my own narcissism, I listen to the Buena Vista concert as if through a fog.

Being an object is tiring. I usually move through the streets completely anonymously, clothed mainly in my own busyness. Now my soul is stuffed away somewhere and I have nothing to feel the music with. I think about my things.

I wonder whether Buena Vista just might be past their prime already.

Love

On the beach, with the usual cast for this place and this season: Christos, my son, my ex-husband, his lover, and the friends who take us in at their house in Lozenets every fall.

There are huge waves. Sometimes they reach ten to twelve feet high. It's hard to get into the sea. Rupen has grown up; handsome, lanky, he skillfully overcomes the waves with his bodyboard. I go in with him. As I stand there admiring him, a wave hits me and mauls me across the bottom. My mouth is full of sand. Panic grips me. I try to find the surface. Fear pounds in my temples. Do I always have to sense life through the terror of death!?

When I finally jump out, I'm a straight tube that furiously inhales-exhales.

I survive this time, too. I manage to overcome the surf and swim on the rounded backs of the waves. A dozen yards ahead, my son glides across the water, stalking the wave, confident and handsome. I don't dare call out. I simply cling to the surface and watch him. My son. Grown up. Independent. I love him more than anything. So much that I simply disappear. I stand there, watch him, and disperse. I am the water, which divides us, which engulfs him. Billions of atoms of love. Whole swimming pools swell up beneath me and the sea sends them to him. Rupen turns and smiles at me.

The wave!

He swims furiously, catches it and lets himself go. He disappears toward its steep side.

I hear his happy shouts.

Alone

Christos is shooting a film in Romania. I'm staying in the mountains for two weeks, waiting for him. I've set up an outdoor studio for myself. For shade, Christos has stretched out ropes and sheets, which flap. The house travels, sails puffed full.

I paint one mirror every day. I paint on massive pieces of wood in the shape of an icon: rounded on top, with small square mirrors mounted in the middle. When I run out of wood, I go down to the carpenter and order thirty more pieces, and in the days while I'm waiting, I get up the courage to revisit the text about Nikula. I'm alone all day, tied to the computer, taking out the monsters of my childhood. I go out only early in the morning to the river for herbs and then I bolt the door. I gradually almost stop eating, I don't shop, I don't change clothes. I don't bathe. I sleep in my old, torn overalls. If I need bread, I bake it. I pick potatoes from the garden and a handful of green beans.

Bread

```
Sift a pound of flour into a wide, flat pan. Shape it
into a volcano and pour into the crater two or three
tablespoons of fresh milk warmed to hand temperature,
along with a pinch of salt, a pinch of sugar, and a
whole packet of dry yeast or half a cube of fresh yeast
(crumbled). Heat up the oven. Set the pan with the volcano
and the rising yeast on its open door so it will be nice
and warm. Once the yeast rises, add more warmed milk—
around a cup, in which an egg, a spoonful of sugar and
a pat of butter as big as a walnut have been dissolved.
Mix it with a wooden spoon at first, in a wooden bowl
if possible. While kneading it, gradually add a quarter
cup of olive oil until the dough stops sticking to your
hands. Then shape the dough into small rolls or buns
```

which can be stuffed with olives, nuts, crushed rosemary or feta cheese, and place them in the baking-dish, once again setting it on the door of the oven to rise for half an hour. After that, glaze the tops of the rolls with egg whites and sprinkle them with caraway, sesame, flax, or poppy seeds. This recipe can also be used for pierogi and other doughy adventures.

The deeper I wade into loneliness, the less I want to come out. The thought of seeing people repulses me. Someone knocks on the door. An actress I know and her new architect fiancé are standing in the dark. I apologize that I'm not able to receive them. They stare at me in amazement. I slam the door in their faces. I call my psychiatrist friend in New York: "Something strange is happening. I have the feeling that I've always been in this house and that I'm never going to leave it."

He asks me in his most soothing voice: "How long have you been there?"

"I don't know."

"When are you leaving?"

"I don't know."

"You're crazy," he shouts. "Set a deadline immediately. Otherwise it's like you're in solitary confinement."

I set a deadline. Christos's return.

He stands in the middle of the square.

So young. Vulnerable. A flower, which has sprung up amidst the tall grass, unsuspected by anyone. I take a deep breath. I close my eyes. I open a space for more joy. The state of storming toward the other after you have been alone for a long time is dangerous. I am unprepared for this passion. What huge spaces to be inhabited.

He just stands there, ready to accept. I start to wonder how I'll keep my hands from pulling and unrolling the thick curls. I step away slightly, even though it is difficult. I hear him telling me about some party, about his friends. I follow the gentle, almost unnoticeable touches along my thigh and think to myself how insufficient that is. I so want him to be overjoyed with me, to see me, goddamn it.

I'm talking about the instant when one soul dives into another. I say: "I'm leaving you. I am leaving you because it's already . . ."

He stops. He turns around, and finally notices me.

I see myself saying it to him. I know that I can't lie. What I'm experiencing is the exact opposite. I don't want to struggle for closeness. Not this way.

After we get home I press against him in the dark room; he immediately falls asleep. I listen to his breathing and since there's no other way I can overflow, I suddenly want to have his child. That way part of him will always belong to me. I will keep him. I imagine some sweet little baby for us to play with on the big bed on the veranda.

All the more so since I'm a few days late and for the first time I'm afraid not that I'm pregnant, but that it will never come again. Suddenly the inability to have a child yawns hollow before me. That delayed, feared privilege of giving life!

Now, suddenly, the horror that I may not possess it, while in fact I always need it only as a possibility.

I'm furious that he has managed to lure me again and again, making me dish out, making me give.

To plunge his hands into my hair, to open his chest wide, to let me reach his very heart, to talk to me, to love me. I want that to happen to me.

It's unbearable when the desires to give and receive are simultaneous.

Does receiving somehow depend on me? Is there something I can do? I ask myself as I slip out of the dark room and throw on a dark blue, half-disintegrated cashmere sweater from some long-since-disappeared lover.

You can love yourself . . . love yourself . . . the bells begin singing, under pressure from the brewing storm. Looks like I've been here by myself too long and far from the others, far from myself as well, and I've again mailed myself off in a letter addressed *To Love, 3 Whenever-He-Comes-Back Street.*

There he is—he's coming back! Always with the look of a gorged bee. Who can blame him for having visited so many flowers? Or else I simply forget that I, too, have drunk nectar, I have been with sunsets—well, fine, so there were no people around, but I wasn't looking for any. Within me dwell so many deserted locales hungry for inhabitation and when I see him, they come to mind.

It hurts so badly, so badly, this cosmic desolation.

Who hurts ... who hurts ... The bells ring on the trees.

Observe the feeling and its opposite ... The Indian bell lays down the bass line.

Wedding

Yesterday I packed away your flowered dress,
so as to forget you
Oh, Venice!

Katya and Flavio Zebonski
invite you to their wedding
on 15 July in the village of Bozhentsi.

Two days before their wedding I finally get divorced. A pure formality: I've already been separated from my husband for four years. The day before going to court, all my strength suddenly leaves me (true, it is over 100 degrees). I lie on the couch, listen to the water from my CD of natural sounds, and sob. I sweat, sob, doze off, drink water, sob again, and doze off again. By the evening I am in a daze.

The next day I put on a white shirt, as if facing the firing squad, go and murmur a few things in front of a judge, and we go our separate ways.

I walk along Patriarch Boulevard and glance around to see what freedom looks like. There are no external signs. I go into Accessoire and buy a necklace of light blue stones, which seems to me the most appropriate color for freedom. On top of it I add a straw hat with the blue's gray nuances, a Queen of England-style hat with a rose in front, and set off for the statue of the Patriarch with my head held high.

These emblems of freedom are marvelous accessories for the dress made especially for the Zebonskis' wedding. It's already ready. How else to muddle through the pre-divorce crisis? Together with my seamstress, Tsenka, we create it from white linen, woven by hand from rough threads; sleeveless, straight to mid-calf length, with a plunging neckline down to my ass in back, while in front the bustline is in the shape of a heart with an unfinished hem. We simply let the threads hang here and there, leaving the cloth as it is, so the dress can be worn even without shoes.

I met Katya in Genoa at a meeting for editors of cultural magazines in Europe, where I was representing *Post Scriptum*. She was doing cultural studies at the Sorbonne and living with a famous Italian photographer who worked for *Vogue*. One day she called up and chirped, "Mandichka, we're getting married!"

The evening before the wedding, they turn up at my place. Katya is sick, out of sorts over the impending event, and he is silent. I chatter all sorts of nonsense at them, feed them. It's not like I have anything to say. I myself have just been driven from the institution of marriage, yet I sense they need me to take care of them. Especially Katya. I lay her down on the bed and massage her head, sing some lullabies, rub scented oil behind her ears and she drifts off.

The next day a caravan of cars sets off for Bozhentsi. When we arrive, Tsveta, a classmate of Katya's, assigns us to various houses. She puts me in the farthest-away house with Moises, a poorly dressed Jewish translator from Genoa, and Tsveta's former lover with his terribly disobedient Wolf. That's the dog's name—Wolf. The owner of the house is attempting to breed ostriches. They stroll around slow and muddy behind a fence, reminiscent of Marquez's angel who fell into the henhouse and was stoned to death by the astonished villagers. It's warm. In the afternoon it rains profusely, and it's like we're in freshly pee-soaked diapers.

We all eat dinner at the local pub: a couple of Croatian conceptual artists, two lovestruck actors from Argentina, one terribly selfish tenor with his fidgety wife—Flavio's sister, who shares his Circassian looks, short and bowlegged from raising horses—and her twenty-year-old daughter, who drags around with her everywhere a two-year-old toddler to whom her mother had given birth before the father left them. They call the baby "Sex Bomb." There's Alessandro the Handsome, Paolo and his brother, sons of the owner of the Inter football club, and some other people, but I don't remember any more. There are also a lot of cats, whose numbers radically decline after Wolf's appearance.

We go back to our houses. I try to read, but the power goes out. The thunder and lightning crack the atmosphere as if we're at a nightclub. Hot humidity swells up from everywhere. Tomorrow people are getting married, getting together, but I'm being attacked by fears, my teeth are chattering and I'm shaking all over: something irrevocable is happening. A kind of fatefulness hangs in the air. I'm stuck at the end of the world. Wolf is howling like the dead, the ostriches are bleating in their pen, while my two neighbors are shaking the house apart with their snoring. I have déjà vu. Collapsing houses above coastal precipices.

That night, in that room with lattice windows facing the river, I am the most ostracized person in the world. The sound of the water doesn't soothe me. An ominous peal of thunder splits the sky and rain comes pouring down. Not drops, but torrents rush over the house. The river beneath it roars frighteningly. I hear choking from the next room. Someone is desperately struggling for a gulp of air. There's no sleep for me. I'm being punished.

Because I'm alone and because I'm not married.

Christos is at a casting call in Rome. Absences.

In the morning the sun is shining as if nothing had happened during the night. Nature's innocence after the night's havoc is astonishing. The light comes and forgives everything. I wasn't the only one who had a nightmarish night. We chalk it up to the storm.

We drink coffee, eat marshmallow cream, and scatter to see what is left of the village after the flood. Everything is still there: the church, the little store, the lovely courtyards, the pub, the irresistible freshness.

A collection of gigantic knives gleams in the noonday sun. Tsveta's jilted lover rushes to buy them, but Moises somehow manages to distract him and they disappear into the pub.

In the afternoon we all head to Gabrovo for the wedding ceremony in the church. In front of the altar Katya is dazzling, at least two heads taller than Flavio; slender with flashing black eyes, in a skintight white lace gown with flowers and a long train. Flavio already has a five o'clock shadow. The priest takes two exquisite crowns but mixes them up, so hers slides down to her nose while his hardly stays on, yet they don't move and don't breathe.

Later when we look at the pictures, we girls are like the queen's ladies-in-waiting: hats, gloves, jewelry. Alessandro, Flavio's handsome friend, has on a red uniform with epaulets—white in the front with gold buttons—and jeans underneath. Slightly Johnnie Walker, except for the indefatigable Italian smile. Paolo's brother, who along with his fifteen-year-old son moved to the Balkan Mountains to live with the Gypsies, had gone to a flea market and outfitted them both with purple suits, yellow shirts, and pointy-toed white shoes. Behind me Moises is whining that he's nervous. He's the only one who admits it. Why we are stressing out so much over this wedding I don't know. I later read in a survey that after divorce, a wedding is the most stressful event. I shush him and pinch him, but he insists—if only we'd had a drink somewhere. Weren't you drinking all morning? *Yes, but it wasn't enough for such an event,* he complains.

Katya and Flavio say "I do" and leave the church in a shower of coins and wheat. The bridal bouquet goes flying!

I don't fight for it.

The wedding night begins slowly, with a heavy dinner served in the courtyard under the sturdy sycamores. Everyone has arrived, including a Lada full of my hard-partying friends who will be the DJs, while Paolo's gift to the newlyweds is a band of dark purple Gypsies. Lamb, wine, toasts to the parents, and light showers. People eat, have fun, the music is fantastic, we dance, the band is cooking. It gradually starts raining harder. No one is surprised. Katya's parents are standing under two separate umbrellas. From a distance they could be mistaken for a pair of concrete deer. The evening rolls on. The rain is now pelting down. People ditch the food. The only way to get through this wedding reception is with dancing, so we give it all we've got. I decide to get rid of the white, far too innocent for this hour, and come back barefoot, wearing only a black slip and the blue symbol of freedom around my neck. They've put up a tent above the Gypsies so that their instruments won't get wet.

"*Kyuchek* yourself!" yells the DJ.[4]

The rain drowns the lamb in the plates.

Flavio's sister radiates unearthly sex. The tenor raises his voice, always hovering above his wife, accusing her of flirting with Alessandro—and how could she not? The Croatians rediscover belly dancing under their European sediment, led, *figurez-vous,* by Paolo's brother and his son, who haven't wasted their time in the Gypsy camp.

During the set breaks, my DJs start in with "Sex Bomb." At two o'clock in the morning the baby Sex Bomb has no intention of sleeping through his uncle's wedding. Barefoot, in muddy diapers, he shakes his big head among the dancers and sings along with Tom Jones: "Sex bomb, sex bomb, baby, sex bomb . . ." Flavio is leading an intense *horo* folk dance. His whole body is shaking. For the first time I see that legendary mix between Arabic, Georgian, Corsican, Greek, and Bulgarian crouching and

---

4   *Kyuchek* is Turkish for "belly dance."

shouting. Nomads, herds, and wolves breathe in his body.

Wolf also howls at the ostriches' pen, tied up and envious of the party. His owner has gotten so drunk from love that he pukes on the sycamores in sharp spasms and falls asleep under the tables. Tsveta also flirts with Alessandro. The warm rain pelts down. Mud. My hair flies around, free of any style. Warmth creeps up from my toes. We dance in anticipation of the Great Flood. This is how you should greet the Flood.

The Argentinians call us one by one to dry land in the restaurant and ask us questions in front of a camera about our feelings on marriage, the newlyweds, and love. We are serious. All of a sudden we must speak. When they drag me over, drenched with my slip sticking to me, covered in mud since I have fallen a few times, I tell them what I think about all those questions in the most nonexistent language, but with absolutely meaningful intonation.

Around five o'clock in the morning the party has reached its climax when one of the concrete deer under the umbrellas moves; Katya's father comes over to me and, with tears in his eyes, begs me to rest for a bit so I won't be sick. I answer him with some cliché and he sits on a stump near the dance floor, his eyes fixed on me.

Before we disperse, a ferocious hunger seizes us. We eat the lamb out of the dishes, fish out the floating vegetables and stumble over Tsveta's jilted lover who has been stewing in his own sauce, an imitation of Marquez's angel in the henhouse. We carry him off before the astonished villagers kill him.

At noon, I'm awakened by beastly squealing, barking, and cackling. I run out on the balcony and see that Wolf has finally broken into the pen and is devouring the ostriches.

The landlord, who clearly made an attempt to protect them, lies brutally bitten and screaming.

Buck naked, Tsveta's jilted lover flashes past me and jumps over the fence. There the Marquez-esque scene reaches new heights, as now there are two muddied angels, the chewed-up ostriches in the form of a classical chorus and Wolf in the role of the astonished villagers, which doesn't prevent him from lunging at both the chorus and the landlord.

I dash down and open the gate to the pen so the Jilted Lover can carry out the wounded. All that wedding angst had to come out somewhere.

Ambulances are called. The landlord's mother throws our luggage out of the house. My suitcase clobbers Moises, who is pissing in the flowers. He staggers a bit, sits down on the steps and asks me longingly if I happen to have a beer. The Jilted Lover locks Wolf in his Jeep, pays for the damage to the birds, and we quickly leave the ostrich ghetto and its astonished inhabitants.

In the café, one by one the personages from the Zebonskis' wedding appear, as if on stage.

The bow-legged sister has cleaned up the Sex Bomb, and he is shining like nature after the rain. The Croatians are excitedly describing their new conceptual project—traveling around China in their own bus—and they invite us all to leave with them right now. Paolo shares intimate details about an upcoming Italian tour by Azis, the Bulgarian transsexual pop icon; he's crazy about our folk stars and has even built a Turkish bath in his house in Milan. The pair of deer sans umbrellas looks a bit livelier than yesterday.

The newlyweds themselves appear amidst applause. Towels full of ice, coffee, beer, sweets, pastries, and sheep's milk are tossed around. Something has happened. We're slightly embarrassed after our unexpected intimacy at the celebration. We don't have a language to speak on the day after the wedding. We have large dark glasses.

Despite my terrible hangover, as I drag myself to the café I notice French signs everywhere and coquettish boxes of purple and red geraniums in the windowsills which, by God, weren't there yesterday. I am just wondering whether after so much emotional intensity these last few days I haven't suffered heavy depersonalization[5] or a personality split, fallen into a dissociative fugue.[6] Katya asks: "Can I just ask where we are, or am I going crazy?" We look at each other over our dark glasses.

"Where are we supposed to be?" Moises didn't quite catch this.

The Argentineans, experienced in Latin American magical realism, give a faint smile: "Wellll, those weren't people, those weren't sideways Latino steps, perhaps we even reached . . ."

"Bullshit," my DJ friends laugh. "As of this morning a Swiss film crew is shooting a movie in Bozhentsi."

"Eh, now that's what I call changing your film," snaps the Jilted Lover.

Tsveta is sitting quietly next to me and projecting some third film

---

[5] Changes in the perception of the external world.

[6] Experience of real events of which the individual has no recollection.

149

into space. Organizing a wedding is no small feat.

The international delegation scatters in all directions. Final good wishes to the newlyweds, and we're off.

On the way back I gather sunflowers.

Free.

Symphonia globulifera

"If you so much as cross this little rope—you see it, right?—here between us, I'm gonna rip your head off and throw it out of the jeep so it can watch us driving away."

"That's not a rope, it's a towel . . ."

"Yes, a towel is separating us now. You have enough room in your half. Don't even think of coming near me," I hiss, eyes narrowed, at six-year-old Toto, with whom I'm sharing the backseat of the jeep. His parents, my old friends Vilyana and Goto, are up front. We are on our way to our next adventure. I came to visit them two days ago in the Caribbean, on the island of Dominica. I don't give a rip about the parents in the front seat. Ever since we got in the jeep, Toto has rubbed, kicked, pressed and climbed on my unhappy, completely burned February body, carelessly exposed to the tropical sun on the very first day. As soon as I land at the airport (a mowed meadow), Goto whisks me off to the jungle in the dark. We walk barefoot. There is nothing prickly, nor any frightening animals. The sky is strewn with fat stars, the river is slow, while the air is the song of a million crickets who don't feel strongly about silence. In the whole racket of the jungle they barely manage to put a dent in "the Bottle Boys," as Goto calls them. Those are frogs that sound like they're thumping on beer bottles in the hollows of the trees. The darkness is light from the inside. We've landed in a magical realm! I bathe ritually as a welcome in the dark waters in which Goto claims there are no crocodiles.

Throwing all caution to the wind, from morning onward I pass the island through my mouth, eating everything I come across. At the market I try the unwashed fruits and vegetables at the stands. Goto, tall as he is, plucks all sorts of fruit for me, of which only mango and guava are familiar, handing me hearts of palm and boiling Indian roots known by the code name *Tanya*. They look a lot like our potatoes, only they're purple.

I expand.

The tropics are so boundless that there is no other way to take them in besides opening up lots of space for them. The fact that this geographical latitude always sickens me speaks to the size of the spaces within me. Amidst this plentitude of flowers and aromas, I break out in all sorts of childhood illnesses. After Australia, I got hit with pneumonias, several in a row. Now upon arrival I puke and shit all night and the whole of the following day. On the morning in question, before we hop in the jeep, I'm already deathly hungry and prepared to commit any manner of villainy for some familiar food. I don't have any except a piece of cheese and a little black bread that I've brought from Bulgaria for the kids. I gobble it down by the refrigerator door without batting an eye. I'm shaking all over. Feeling better, I get in the jeep with Toto. He has completely run wild. Not that his father wasn't wild as a kid, but Toto has truly outdone him, keeping in mind how everything grows here in the tropics.

Goto, beaten regularly by his mother until he finally learned to play cello, has decided to not force or limit his son in any way. As a result, Mowgli is now sitting next to me. Beautiful and gifted with unusual intuition, but difficult to tolerate within a radius of less than thirty feet, he has no sense of boundaries. Still completely swathed in Sofia fog and prohibitions, I look upon this scourge and wonder how I will survive it. We blaze through banana plantations and bamboo forests along the seashore. From the other side of the towel, Toto follows me from the corner of his eye. I am on guard as well. Behind us in the far back seat are Rebecca—the kids' babysitter—and Ilé, Toto's three-year-old sister with brown ringlets and a mischievous expression.

Ilé is an empiricist. She insists on gathering her own rich experience. She walks around the tropics with complete self-confidence, shrugging one little shoulder and mumbling something to herself, always engrossed in some mission of her own. "Ilé," her father says, "don't go near the waves, they'll sweep you away!" Ilé turns around, hears him, and heads straight for the waves. She stops at a perfect spot for getting swept away. A few seconds later, a strong wave mauls her in the surf. Goto stands and watches Ilé flail in the foam. With a few leaps, he has pulled her out and is looking her over as she coughs and spits out saltwater. "Didn't I tell you they would sweep you away?" he whispers to her as he snuggles her in a towel. "Yes, they'll sweep me away," Ilé confirms, and throws up.

What a childhood! They live above a virgin beach with palms and a crystal-clear river that empties into one end of the bay. They gather coconuts, avocados, guavas, mangoes, lemons, grapefruit, and bananas from the nearby trees. Goto comes back from the sea with fish.

"My sweat smells like grapefruit, maaan, like grapefruit," he says, always adding "man" at the end like the Rastas. Toto and Ilé play with the children of the Indians and the Rastafarians. They sleep and eat wherever dreams and hunger catch up with them.

I was seven when Goto was born. He was like my doll—I dragged him around with me all day, singing made-up songs. He has an incredible ear, he graduated from music school and left to study at Berklee, married Vilyana there—a talented violin player—and had two kids.

After the towers fell, Goto was done with America. He rented out his house in Boston and moved to Dominica, and while Vilyana hops airplanes to play around the world, Goto has ditched the cello and wrenches sounds from whatever he can get his hands on.

Goto and Vilyana built their Dominican house out of stone and wood. It curves along the trees, with big door-windows that are closed only when it rains. The whole house is open toward the ocean. The problem of electricity is solved by a portable windmill, which automatically falls to the ground when a hurricane whips up. For washing and bathing they use rainwater, which runs off the roof into a cistern, while they draw drinking water from a nearby spring.

When the rainy season begins in May the family returns to Bulgaria for the summer, returning to the tropics in October. After several years on the island, Vilyana is looking around for civilization, since the children's education is imminent. Besides that, several expensive violins have dried out on her, thanks to the climate, as she practices under the palm trees before embarking on her next world tour.

We travel along the lone, narrow road along the sea. We are going to the rainforest.

Christopher Columbus discovered the island on a Sunday, hence the name Dominica. When the Spanish queen asked him what the island looked like, he took a sheet of paper, crumpled it up and threw it on the floor. That's exactly what it looks like. There's a high mountain in the center, which slants steeply in places while sloping toward the sea in others. The population is made up of Indians, who sailed there from the Orinoco Valley, and blacks, brought there as slaves first by the French and later by the English. The flora and fauna are whatever managed to fly and swim over from South America. Everything that rolls drowned along the way. Here they speak a strange sort of English and end phrases with "man." This "manly" island has three climates: moderate down by the shore, never getting hotter than 86° or colder than 77°F; tropical in its northern part; and rainforest on the mountain, over a thousand feet above sea level. There it rains almost every half hour, and afterward the sun shines softly amidst the steam. Dominica has 365 rivers, some of them hot.

We enter an enormous nature preserve. There are signs in front of the rarer trees, giving their Latin names. I read them out loud into my microphone, which I do not part with because I want to make a new ambient disc of the tropics. The rubber trees tower like gigantic cathedrals. I'm thinking of not using that word anymore, because here everything is gigantic: the parrots, the birds of paradise, the flowers on the trees, the clarity of the rivers, the coral, the leaves on the ficus. Just try to tell me God isn't on the side of abundance!

The only insufficient thing is the barely audible whistling of a bird. Two notes, which it holds for a long time: one after the other, provoking a sharp yearning for something beloved that has gotten lost somewhere in these forests. It'll be enough for me just to record Mr. Whistler. I could listen to his searching for hours. I catch the sound of him here and there, but he keeps slipping away from me, or else the kids are shouting.

Goto likes the game "say the name of the tree." I record him drawling out the Latin names of every rare species along our path. At one point a huge tree appears before us, all full of hollows, birds and flowers. Goto sounds it out: SYMPHONIA GLOBULIFERA. "Symphonia globulifera," we repeat, enchanted; "Symphonia globulifera!" shout the children, running back and forth.

We're walking to some waterfall. I lag behind the group, stalking Mr. Whistler, but the forest is silent. I hurry to catch up with them.

On the path, Ilé is writing something with a stick, talking to herself in her own language. I squat down next to her and listen. The meaning ripples out, liquefied. I carefully place the microphone under her. She's naming the leaves and sticks with some words of her own, but she sees the microphone and shuts up. She looks at it intensely. Then at me. Then at the microphone again. I sit there, patiently waiting for her to get carried away in her monologue. Ilé deals me such a healthy slap from close up with her strong little arm that I plunk down on the path. She is serious. Anger grips me and I smack her back, which makes her plunk down as well. We look at each other for a few seconds, during which I am suddenly gripped by the horror that any second now she'll start bawling. What am I going to tell her parents? Ilé sees my panic, doesn't hesitate to take advantage of it and pumps up the bagpipes. Soon Goto bounds out of the bushes, followed by Vilyana and Toto. Ilé is screaming bloody murder, while they, frightened, ask what happened. I confess. Goto picks her up, kisses her, and a second later Ilé is already laughing with a tear hanging from her cheek, while I, ashamed, don't dare look them in the eye.

"How could a woman of your age hit a little child?" they yell over one another.

I want to disappear into the leaves, when they start giggling like mad. Vilyana whispers: "I'm like you, too; I don't let them get away with it just because they're kids."

I remember that back when Ilé was seven months old, I tried to record her cooing, but she saw the microphone and clammed up. I crawled next to her for hours on end, but to no avail.

Ilé has her reasons for not wanting to give me her language.

OK. Let's at least hope that Mr. Whistler will give me his.

In the evening on the terrace in front of the house, we get together to jam. Rastas show up with their drums; we take out all our instruments and start building on the wind and surf. I've turned on my equipment. Afterward I play it back so we can hear the recording. There's nothing there. It hasn't recorded a single sound. I'm sure it was recording, I checked with the headphones several times. Not a sound. Through the bells hung on the lemon tree, I hear the laughter of Ryokan, the wanderer-poet:

> The thief
> left it—
> the moon in the window.[7]

The children are falling asleep in the hammocks under the trees. Rebecca tells me her life story. She's seventeen. She has run away from her home in Iowa. Her stepfather started having sex with her when she was twelve. She told her mother, but her mother didn't believe her. Rebecca

---

[7] From a Zen Buddist poem.

does yoga for two hours every morning and then meditates. She drinks some infusion to cleanse her body and soul of all that. She's been living with Vilyana and Goto for two years, taking care of their children. They are now building a studio for her at the end of the yard. We talk until the sky grows pink.

I am awakened by Ilé's songs, coming from the toilet: "Doomberday-doomberday—niiiiine raaaabbits . . . doomberday-doomberday—niiiiine raaaabbits."

"Niiiiiiine raaaabbits," Toto also yells from the yard. I get up, unrested and talked out, and decide not to speak until evening. I write on a slip of paper: *nine rabbits*. I give it to everyone who wants to talk to me.

We breakfast on sweet grapefruit. I get my beach bag ready and head off down the path with Rebecca when from the house we hear ecstatic shouts: "Frank! Frank is here!" Rebecca tosses down her bag and runs back.

I call after her, forgetting that I'm being silent, "Who is this Frank, anyway?" but she doesn't reply, she's downright flying. I take our bags and shuffle back up the hill.

Frank is an American who is boycotting civilization. He is creating an alternative world. He lives high in the rainforest, without electricity and running water, with his several wives; he has ten children, he builds himself clay houses, he buys almost nothing from the stores; he makes everything himself, including toys for the kids. They grow marijuana. A handsome man, with his latest baby in his arms, with beautiful women around him and little Rastas—as lively as Toto and Ilé. With a wide smile, Frank hands out joints as thick as thumbs and everyone flops down in the hammocks.

Goto grabs one and drags me off toward the sea. I toss aside the bags except for my little backpack, in which I have a scarf, glasses, a hat and some water, and we set off. "A change of plans," he winks at me; "I can't not share the Coral Pool with you." We take hits as we walk. I'm silent. He tells me about Frank, who is seriously concerned about the world's ecology and for that reason has decided to live his way. He won't even accept Toto's books for his children. Everything he makes takes him a long time, but he's not hurrying. There's nowhere to hurry to.

Strange things start happening to me, thanks to the ganja. We climb down the steep cliffs. I feel myself clinging to the slope at the most unbelievable angles without any fear at all.

The Coral Pool is naturally carved out of the cliffs a little above sea level, its bottom covered with pieces of white coral smoothed by the waves. The water in the little pool is about two feet deep and is constantly draining until the ninth wave goes overboard, filling it up once again. It's the ideal refuge on a stormy, windy day like today. We lie on the bottom. The sea is visible before us and from time to time the froth of the ninth wave gently spills over. I'm seriously baked, even though I only took three hits. My desire for silence keeps growing, but Goto has started chattering away. I relax onto the water and flow out with it. When I reach the bottom, the ocean pours in and I am once again on the surface. I like this game. Goto senses that I'm no longer hearing him and shuts up. I take a deep breath and exhale slowly until I fall to the bottom under the water. I stay there, quiet and empty. I look at the sky through the water. Until now, I've only managed this degree of centered calmness during meditation a few times. Peace. Homecoming. The water runs out; a new wave comes and lifts me. With its inrush, I take a breath again. I exhale and stay on the bottom for an eternity. I don't need air. I don't need anything. I fuse with the rhythm of the ocean. I breathe only with the ninth wave. I don't know how many hours I spend in this up-and-down rocking between the bottom and the surface. At one point, unexpectedly, while I'm on the bottom, an old fear surfaces: that Goto will violate me. Fear that now, defenseless as I am, he could do something to me that I don't want. I stay with this. I observe. Reason tells me *Come on, are you nuts, this is your childhood friend, the kid you grew up with, how could you think that?* But the fear stays there and grows stronger. I know that drugs open up my paranoia. During the European train trip in Minsk, after half a shot of vodka with hashish, I was driving disintegrating trains straight downward. Clear enough—fear of death. But this? Could I have been raped and not know it? I search. There's no memory. I hadn't heard of anything like that in the family. I watch.

Finally, the next autumn, I receive the answer accidentally while talking to Sara, my mother's younger sister who lives in Germany. She tells me that when she was thirteen and my mother was fifteen, Nikula and Boris had gone to sell some piece of land along the Danube. They had taken the baby Maruna with them. They left my mother and Sara with four-year-old Klement in Dimitrovgrad, where they were living at that time after coming back from Czechoslovakia. The house was on the outskirts of the city. One evening—it was the dead of winter—the firewood ran out. My mother stayed at home with Klement, while Sara set out into the forest, as in a classic fairytale. In the woods, eight boys raped her. My aunt doesn't have any memory of how she got home; some people must have found her. I ask my mother about it, but she pushes that story aside, claiming that my aunt made it up. There was a trial and the rapists paid damages to Nikula. My aunt says that most likely with this money and what they made from selling that property, Nikula began building the house in Nesebar and they all moved there for the fresh air.

When I hear this story, I understand why my mother cried all night when I started going out with my friends and why she stood by the window until I made it home. I recognize her terror of things that happen beyond the home, and her fear of every sign of my femininity. This anxiety murmurs somewhere deep within me. But there on the bottom, on top of those coral tiles, I am puzzled as to where this fear of my own vulnerability is seeping out from. We get up. We move over to Pointe Baptist, a place jutting out into the sea next to the Coral Pool, where there are trees. I carefully wrap myself up in my scarf and lie on the sand for who knows how many more hours, stuck motionless between reality and something more infinite. At a certain point, Goto asks me in a tortured voice, "Do you have any water?" We guzzle down all I have and I look at him, amazed, because despite so much experience with ganja, he had not thought to bring water. But I guess weed is incompatible with the future tense. Its effect finally begins to wear off; we swim in the ocean and we go back to the house, slow and soft, where we find the others in the same condition. Everyone is hungry. Rebecca whips up some curry sauce with boiled *tanya* roots.

The next morning, we traipse over to Champagne Beach, where bubbles hiss from the cliffs since the volcanic activity on this island has never ceased. Warm water with a whiff of sulfur gushes into the sea. The fish here are yet more colorful and whimsical. On the bottom, there are coral pots out of which, if you rap on them, shoot thousands of little blue fish. I've seen that somewhere before.

Goto teaches me how to even out the pressure so I can dive deeper down to the other wonders. I try, but my ears fill irrevocably with water and I give up.

In the evening, we leave this heavenly place to go back up to the rainforest. The sun slowly sets. We go to the warm river. Its bed is red from sulfur. The water is 104° Fahrenheit. Somebody has split bamboo stalks for showerheads; here and there thick streams splash from the rapids. We grow quiet in the warm river. Blacks and Indians with towels tossed over their shoulders swim out of the jungle dusk and say: "OK!" with their hands up in a sign of goodwill. The stars rain down on us from above. It's cozy in this forest. Bottles fit snugly into the hollows of the trees. Now that I'm wet and naked, sans microphone, Mr. Whistler calmly shouts out his tune. Downstream, the songs of the island's inhabitants ring out. I am simultaneously lost and found. I flow toward the ocean.

As we get dressed, the kids are already screaming from hunger. Vilyana gives them water and some rolls, which they gnaw on in the car on the way back, falling asleep piled on top of each other. We also nibble at these mysteriously delicious rolls (we buy them from the Indians up on the mountain) and once we reach the house, we hurl ourselves gratefully down on the bed in the cool breeze from the sea.

Then my agony begins.

My ear has been festering from the day's balancing acts and is now throbbing. I know this pain in my head well; it's an old friend. It accompanied me closely throughout my whole childhood. It begins with a slight muffling and climaxes in a sharp pinching that leaves me shrieking.

We are miles from any civilization. I don't have any painkillers. Everyone is exhausted from the day.

I go to the kitchen. The pain and I take a good long look at each other. Someone has cranked up the crickets to the max. They are shoving an enormous cupboard in my ear. I know that I can't allow myself even a second of self-pity. I light the gas burner and pour a little olive oil in the frying pan. I pound a couple of cloves of garlic with all my might and let them sizzle a bit in the warm olive oil over a very low flame. I go outside and gather a few round stones the size of my palm. I set them in a pot of water to boil. I hurry, since the pain is gathering speed. Soon I will only be able to howl.

I fall to the floor of the kitchen, rocking back and forth, whimpering quietly. Mine alone. I cannot share it. My pain. I can't even grab it by the hand. I hold my head. I wait for the stones to boil and for the olive oil to leach the antibiotics from the garlic.

I close my eyes and imagine that I am inhaling light and love from the painful place and exhaling the bad stuff. I try to concentrate my entire inner attention on my inflamed canal. I imagine it healthy and smooth. The pain rages. I barely manage to drip the olive oil in my ear, plug it with a paper napkin, wrap the hot stone in a towel and press it on top. Thus brought low, I beg the pain to pass me by. Warm stones the whole night. I change them and breathe from the painful place. Toward morning I've drifted off. I am awakened by *doomberday, doomberday, niiine raaabbits*—that bathroom ritual of Ilé's. The pain has subsided. A large stake has been driven in my ear, buzzing dully and unexpectedly. No more adventures.

But how will I leave the day after tomorrow with this ear, if my ears can't pop and equalize the pressure on the airplane?

Goto brings over some ninety-year-old grandfather, who he tells me is the local healer, and the rest of them set off on an excursion to the mountain. He sits in the wicker chair next to me. His face has been carved by time. His hair is hidden by a colorful, Rasta-style crocheted hat. He smokes weed and doesn't speak. From time to time he mutters something incomprehensible or lays some sermon on me, peppered with Biblical parables, and then spaces out again. I do the same. Every half-hour he brings me some hot stone from the street, so the pain can pass onto it. Other times he simply lays his hand on my ear. His hands are enormous and as wrinkled as his face. With slow movements, he makes tea from some leaves. His toothless mouth whispers: "Poef, bay leaf, lemongrass . . ." Gradually, the huge stake in my ear disappears. I get used to his presence. He's here, but it's as if he's not. I fall asleep, I wake up, the old man is always there next to me.

By evening there is no trace of the pain. Only a slight deafness remains. Upon leaving, he smiles, wags a long finger in front of my face, and says dramatically: "If you love yourself, you will do nothing wrong to yourself!"

I kiss his hand in gratitude.

After the excursion, the group is ravenous. I am, too. The pain has opened up a space. They are carrying bags of avocados. Rebecca has raised a new crop of peanut, soy, and lentil sprouts. Vilyana makes steamed basmati rice and salad from the avocados and sprouts.

Sprouts

Best from lentil, peanut, and soy. Soak the seeds in water separately for one night. Then place them in a strainer and wash them with running water three times a day so they don't go sour. When they sprout, they are ready for consumption.

Rice with Sprouts

Boil basmati rice (two cups of water to one cup of rice) along with finely chopped hot peppers for several minutes on high, then reduce the heat and simmer covered for another three minutes. Just before it is ready, add fresh basil, sprouts, sprigs of lemongrass (which will be removed later), two cloves of finely chopped garlic, a spoonful of curry, a can of coconut milk, three tablespoons of olive oil, and salt to taste. Stir it up carefully. Turn off the heat after five minutes and let the rice stand covered for another five minutes with the new ingredients.

After dinner, I take Ilé and we lie in the big hammock on the veranda. She is in a quiet phase: flopped down on her back on top of me, looking at the sky, sunk in silence. At such moments, I am sure that she is Buddha.

Toto is drifting off in the neighboring hammock, exhausted from the outing.

One by one, the parents take out instruments, their ethnic treasures—gourds, strings of peppers, seeds, maracas, African thumb pianos, Moroccan drums, the Rastas show up—and the music begins, now growing louder, now pulling back, depending on the surges of energy. Sometimes one person is really active and the others quietly hold the drone; then the jamming thins out, leaving only the Bottle Boys and the surf down below.

Vilyana rocks the hammock out of habit. The stars hang so low above us that when she rocks us harder they get tangled in Ilé's curls.

I feel the warmth of her little body on me and hug her. We breathe together.

We listen to SYMPHONIA GLOBULIFERA ...

Red Dress 2

In the spring, after my trip to Dominica, slightly euphoric from the generosity of the tropics, I decide to do a reading of selected works from my books with the poet Toma Markov. A year earlier, we had read together on Radio France Internationale. The audience went nuts, calling in, wanting more. So we start meeting in his little kitchen, selecting the poems. He wants me to print them up for him on a scroll, he wants his cash in advance. In short, everything just as it should be.

He sees himself dressed in my red velvet dress. That same red velvet dress. He has this fantasy of me putting on boxing gloves and beating the shit out of him at some point as he reads.

But what is the point of this reading, since I don't write poetry anymore? My poems have stood silent for years, unheard, because I have no voice for my own things. Or so I think. Now look, when Markov recites them—then they sound good. They seem loved. He has a sense for rhythm and for the stage. He knows them by heart!

I send messages to everyone I can think of: "Come to the performance *Tomato—Soup—Toma Markov Reads Manda* at the Red House. Don't forget to bring your spoons!" I think it is precisely that line that attracts so many people. For two days, my mother and I make tomato soup. Fifteen gallons of it, following the monastery recipe. We pour it into two-gallon water jugs. I put a pedestal in front of the entrance to the hall and toss a Socialist-era hot plate with a big green pot on top. My sister has stuffed her scorching cleavage into my corset, which is at least three sizes too small, so her endless tits spill over the top. She smiles sweetly and dishes up soup for the arriving guests.

The people slurp their soup, talk quietly amongst themselves, and wait for the performance to start. It looks a bit like a funeral.

There's a problem inside the hall. The percussionist, who is supposed to create a background beat for the reading, can't get his electronic drums working. There's no rhythm. Markov is shuffling back and forth, fanning out the red dress. Since he can't button it up, we've bought him red boxers.

So from top to bottom, the fifty buttons cohabit with the secondary characteristics of his masculinity. Barefoot and anxious, he won't let anyone into the hall. Good thing we've got soup galore. The performance could easily end here, because we've seen each other, chatted a bit, and had a bite to eat.

But the doors open. People hand over their tickets and toss their empty soup cups into the trash can. Christos sits quietly in the front row behind the camera. I sit next to him, wearing a black skirt with white polka dots and a red feather boa, which I just got as a gift. The hall is full. Markov is facing the corner. We quiet down with David Lynch: a red hall, red light, a man in a red velvet floor-length gown and red gloves up to his elbows—we made gloves from the sleeves due to his muscles. Suddenly Markov whirls around theatrically and announces: "I am Manda."

There is no getting out of this now.

He starts reading. He snuffles, mumbles, and mutters something under his nose. Yet he still decisively rips off what has already been "read." He strolls around the stage, paper fluttering in his wake, his voice growing ever softer. The whole audience disappears and transforms into a hopelessly pricked-up, progressively deafened ear. Yet what joy when we manage to make out some word! I see my father and his deaf retinue twisting helplessly in their seats.

I am frozen. SHAME. I can't believe it—there's no trace of his ballsy reading. Markov skips through the text, reading a line here and there, mumbling something to himself and ripping off what has been "read."

We sink. I can't do anything. The curse of the red dress has mauled both of us. Since he's crazy enough to play me, let him see what it's really like. The drummer stands on stage in front of his mute electronic drums, watching the show from the other side, having fallen into an ecstatic stupor.

I could get up and lay into Markov in the corner. Toss him out of the hall with a good spanking. I could grab a vat of soup and pour it over his head. Put on the boxing gloves—as he himself fantasized—and beat the shit out of him, until his blood spills over the red dress.

But how can a person beat himself?

In *Fight Club*.

But in this case it is simple enough just to sit there.

So that's what I do: speechless, numb, completely detached from that which is happening. So that's how I miss the unique opportunity Markov gives me—to be rid of myself. While he pretends to be Manda, I, as the boozer Markov, could actually commit a whole raft of stupidities. I could get the crowd to do the wave or make them read the poems with him as the audience. So many things come to mind. Always afterward. Do I have the right to afterward? I don't.

So I dangle there, neither myself nor someone else.

The familiar discomfort in defending my territory. I'll make a fool of myself if I show how angry I am! I keep my mouth shut and wait for a miracle.

Certainly, the two most natural things don't occur to me—to get up and herd Markov into the audience, give him a bowl of soup, wrap him up in something and afterward read the end of the scroll myself. Maybe some trauma of his own came over him, but why on top of my poems?

I don't think of this. There in that moment I am anger, affront and confusion. I start yelling: "Speak up! Read more clearly!"

Behind me, indignant voices second me: "We can't hear!"

Good God, how polite we all are. But Markov as Manda is deaf as well as mute. Then I realize that there are sheets with poems next to me, which, according to the script, we need to fold into swallows and let fly away. I crumple up the paper and toss it at the reader. Next to me, others start throwing as well. Christos, as pedantic as can be, keeps filming. Things as they are.

The scroll finally ends. Markov hauls me out of the front row and now we're taking a bow. Shame disciplines. Throws you into the cliché. It bends you.

I give in. For an instant there is a flash of hope—if I act like this was my favorite reading ever, maybe they won't notice. Just like in a nightmare, you keep hoping to wake up and that it was all a dream.

The audience applauds. I am definitively implicated.

Tomato soup or swallowing a frog.

Hungry viewers fight for more soup on their way out. They say things to me. Somebody makes off with a two-gallon jug for some shelter. A famous critic obligingly mentions that she likes that technique for sharpening attention, and it was precisely because of this that she managed to hear a few ingenious phrases. People are crawling on the floor, gathering up poems so they can read them.

I sit down on a radiator. With the boa around my neck. I toast my beaver, which was absolutely frozen with horror, and hold the cup of warm soup that my sister hands me.

Christos didn't think to film the distribution of the soup, how lame. That alone is completely sufficient as a performance. If only I'd told them *Look, guys, the poems are in the soup, I boiled them along with the tomatoes. Here's the poetry. Take it internally.*

How can I not love Failure!

There is a surety, a rock-bottom sincerity to it. Failure as the solder, joining the bombastic events of our lives and so important for the conversation of being with itself.

As I write this piece and delouse my desktop, I open an invitation for an art action by Katya Zebonska, who triumphantly curates throughout Europe. The project is intended for Tirana. The concept reads: "The party depends on the people and their ability to forget their identity!"

It could've been an amazing party of tomatoes, tits, an audience strained to bursting and a mute, nude Markov in a gaping red dress. What material gone to waste!

But how can I forget myself precisely when I'm trying to remember who I am?

Post-tomato

After my red failure, I swear to never let anybody read my stuff again and to stand up for what I do. A series of readings ensue in which I definitively recover from my childhood shame of getting up in front of an audience.

First, I take part in a forty-eight-hour reading of Joyce's *Ulysses* at the Red House. I sit in an exquisite green armchair, specially done-up in a yellow taffeta gown fitted at the waist and flared to below the knee à la Jackie Kennedy, with black eyeliner, a bun, pearls and beige, low-cut shoes like my mother's. I read the part of the book assigned to me four times longer than expected; I flirt, throw my legs up on the armchair, take outrageous liberties with the pauses, flash my lingerie, twirl the pearls, lick my lips. I'm obnoxious.

To shore up the newly awakened attitude within me toward performing, I organize a series of literary readings and, along with four other women, I read my piece about PMS at the Red House amidst red pillows scattered on the floor, while a big teapot full of herbs and cinnamon puffs away behind me. The piece is pretty heavy and long. That's why I count on suspense. I chop it up with the noise of two toasters, which spit out toast by the minute, and I moon the audience in fishnet stockings and a red dress with white polka dots—I take the slices out and put in new ones. Then I read again. It smells like toasted bread, like Grandma's kitchen.

After the reading, people flop down on the pillows, stretch their hands out toward the toasters as around a campfire, monstrously hungry; they root around in the basket with texts for more bread, toasting, buttering (drooling from the smell), and drinking tea. We talk about literature and other things.

I could now make a buck or two in a peep show if need be.

Wellfuckitallanyway.

The Mad Hatter

I'm at the Apartment, talking with Mariët Meester, a Dutch writer I grew close to on the literary train. She has come to Sofia to write her next book in peace, while her husband, a conceptual artist, puts on an exhibit at the Sofia City Gallery. In the evenings we make the rounds. The Apartment is a private club. It's like being at home, except that people are coming and going around the clock, writing on their laptops, rolling around on the sofas with design and fashion magazines, drinking, smoking. Techno, house, and chill-out tick away in the background. If you come at three in the afternoon, they've got their right legs crossed over their left; in the evening, the same people, only now their left legs are over their right. Then, however, I was there for the first time. It's already three in the morning. We stretch out on the pillows. She is so delicate, with white freckled skin and red hair. Her writing is brutal. You can have marvelous conversations with her about literature, about your innermost self. I'm tormented by doubts as to whether I'll ever be able to write again. I'm afraid that I've closed myself off to it forever. Mariët lives only through writing. If someone looked at us from the side, he'd think we were confessing our love to each other, which in a certain sense is exactly the case.

"Don't you understand? If I don't write, it's like I'm not here. I don't exist. I've set a trap for myself, Mariët, I've reduced myself to one of my ideas. I'm here to write, and since that hasn't been happening for some time now, that means I'm nothing. But otherwise I keep up the act, I build up an image. But, in fact, I don't exist. In my own eyes. I try not to be like my mother, yet I fall into her trap. She didn't manage to make her dream of becoming a singer come true. Since she's not the one thing she thinks she is, it means she doesn't exist. What monstrous fear of life, disguised in the justification—*since I'm not a singer, I don't exist.* She isn't there for adventures, for boldness. The fact that she is unique, that she creates beauty out of everything she touches, that she's wonderful, how can she be blind to that? How can she have blinded herself?"

"I would ask you the same thing," Mariët tries to slip in, but I keep going:

"So that's why I have to express myself for her, too, now. But even if I pull off miracles, she still won't be satisfied, because it isn't happening to her, with her. She doesn't own it. Hence her terrible appetite for MORE, which has become mine. Exactly this 'more, come on, give more' deprives me of joy . . ."

"How can you possibly have such low self-esteem when you do so many things? Important things. I mean, you were one of the most interesting people on that literary train."

"When the things I do have no particular resonance, it doesn't matter whether they exist or not . . ."

Mariët can see how her husband's installations have sunk into total silence after the preview. How can I explain to her that here the cultural context is like shifting sands—it can swallow up so much without ever giving anything back.

Next to me, the owner of the Apartment is struggling with a computer. I ask him, "So how do you become a member here?"

Without turning around, he mumbles: "With time, but time is running out." And with that, he disappears toward the kitchen.

He soon returns; I've sunk my teeth in, so I ask again. He glances at me sideways and says, "You have to be an artist to be a member of the Apartment."

Silence.

"Are you an artist?"

"I don't know," I stutter. "I've got some books."

A blank. I cannot for the life of me remember what should define me as an artist.

"I do performances and I've got a CD."

He looks at me suspiciously with his watery green eyes, sees that something isn't quite right with me and suddenly barks: "So what's your name?"

I hate saying my name.

"Manda."

"From *Post Scriptum* magazine?"

"Yes."

"I published *Sax!* During the same time," he flushes, gets up and leaves the room, without answering my question. Fucking Mad Hatter.

Mariët pensively says: "MORE—here's where your inability to see what you create comes from. More kills. More erases what has been done. You create something. The fruits of your energy. At that moment the work decides to appear through you. You take responsibility for it. You are responsible for that which you create, Manda. Do you get it? Nihilism is just another way of hiding from yourself."

"That's true—I don't dare take responsibility for my stuff. That's why it always seems to me that I don't have anything, I don't exist and I always have to prove myself. This uncertainty is old. They never want me. I don't know where to go, but I've also lost the path toward myself. That's why I'm so vulnerable to others' doubts."

I find the owner in the kitchen. "Will you explain to me what's going on here?"

"Time . . . time is running out."

Dragons

You are the travelers, you are the goal,
You are the path and you are the origin.

The rainforest on the island of Dominica. A husky blond man sits on a sun-warmed slope. I see his blue eyes, the same color as the sea standing up all around. A little girl is playing near him. It's damp. It has just rained. Suddenly a huge red snake bursts into the picture, swimming through the air. I think to myself *Oh God, just don't let it strangle the man*. And that's exactly what happens—it wraps itself around his neck. The man struggles frantically to take a breath. The child is screaming and cannot help him. Finally, the man manages to escape from the snake. I run and run until I reach my mother's kitchen, where there are other women as well. I'm crying, shaking, and saying over and over: "I can't, I can't, I can't stop being afraid of that brutal female archetype! It terrifies me!" They fuss around me, calming me and hugging me.

I wake up.

I think about the women in my family and their cruelty toward men. Their cruelty toward their own selves. I want to make peace with myself. I need tenderness, compassion, and gratitude.

I get up, determined not to allow that dragon to destroy anything more. To destroy me. I start giving thanks to myself from morning on, to smother outbursts of my inner cruelty, but the nightmares continue.

I'm riding in a taxi with some man in an exotic city with parrots in the trees. I take his hand, but he pulls away and tells me that he doesn't like that. I feel superfluous.

I wake up and wonder where this theme in its different variations comes from, since there is nothing to spark it during the day.

A few days later, I have another dream: he's cold again. I've gone to pick him up from some hovel. While he gathers up his things, I stand by a swollen river. Vegetables I have bought spill and roll on the ground. A woman marvels at the basket full of basil, dill, and sage and begs me to give her some. The river overflows its banks, the people huddle together frightened; I sit down in the middle of the roaring water on a big stone and play the theme from Shostakovich's *Concerto for Trumpet, Piano and Orchestra* on a trumpet. I'm really good. The man piles clothes and things in the car. He is naked. Handsome. He puts on bright yellow swimming trunks, puts on a bikini top and struts around. His legs are so shapely that he could pass for a woman. We go to a hotel. He lays out his things on the bed—nice clothes, pretty little boxes, jewelry. He packs his bags. He's leaving for somewhere new and interesting. He is completely absorbed in his things. I sit and watch him off to the side. I am not part of his world. He doesn't care. I ask him why he's acting like this. He replies: "Because you're an old bag."

"You're the one pushing me into that role. It's best for this to end."

"Well, yeah, the less drama, the better," he agrees.

I know that whether I go outside or stay, either way I'll suffer terribly. I sit. There, nailed to the spot, I envy and hate him, want to kill.

I open my eyes. It's five-thirty in the morning.

It's cold as a tomb. I get up. I stand in the middle of the dark living room in my pajamas, trembling. How many rejections can I stand? I'm furious. How long will envy of other people's lives and a feeling of abandonment haunt my dreams?

How can I defend myself, since in my dream I have no choice?

I remember just one time when I succeeded, and that was a dream about an enormous man who tormented me. I told him to wait a minute. I ran, got a chair, set it in front of him, climbed up on it and slapped him hard across the face. I woke up and made the decision to leave my husband.

Now no one is openly tormenting me, except perhaps myself.

I go back to get some more sleep and order myself to understand the meaning of this nightmare at all costs. When I wake up at nine o'clock, there are several phrases hanging in the air: *Take care of yourself. It's not that others' lives are so interesting and full of colorful things, but that your life has been emptied of content. You've become too responsible and predictable.*

I wonder what the practical dimension of those words could possibly be on an ordinary day: six hours in the office, then a lecture for students at the Art Academy, in the fashion department, on the topic "To Be and To Appear," and after that . . . I don't flop down on the couch, but head down Shishman Street. I spend. I buy myself cheerful clothes fit for Pippi Longstocking, have a drink, and shoot the shit with friends in the cafés.

In the months after that answer, my life takes on color. I start going to improvised dance class, where we're rags and we wipe the floor with our bodies. Then belly dance—another little door to dance. I discover a yoga teacher—a tiny Indian man folds me in half like a slice of bread and walks on top of me. I hand him the responsibility for the torture, so that I can play a little, too. I breathe more freely and have strength. After working in the office I go out in the evening. I stop dreaming about being superfluous and cruel female dragons! This weakness is present in my day, so it isn't necessary to shove it off into dreams. I start caring for my innermost self.

I sit in silence, observe my breath, and practice gratitude toward existence. I begin receiving love, gifts, and gratitude. From everywhere.

Steam

This morning I put on a lama's mantras, so calming that I don't feel like struggling with anything at all. I sit and cannot tear myself away from the sofa. I've forgotten my just-brewed cup of coffee in front of the window.

She makes coffee so that afterward she can forget it somewhere because, in fact, she doesn't feel like drinking it. She loves the smell . . .

The steam rising in front of the morning sun. It loses its density in all directions—soft and transparent. I stand enchanted before the brilliance of the red cup of Japanese porcelain with its vertical coiffure of water molecules.

I recall my psychodrama group: we do an exercise in which each one of us must identify her source of energy. The image of a light ceramic cup with little roses pops up for me—hand-drawn, full of hot tea. Afterward, in groups, we share that which recharges us and create a common story.

Our group plays out the story of a person who is sitting in his favorite old leather armchair, stroking his cat, eating chocolate on a sunny terrace in front of the house and sipping tea from a cup with tiny roses.

I play the steam rising above the tea.

At 46

She has a well-kept body, with a slightly fluffy little stomach. Unlike before, she likes it a lot. She loves holding her small feet in her hands. Sometimes she gets so wrapped up in staring at her hands as they firmly grasp the steering wheel that she almost crashes. All this ecstasy isn't just to cover up the fears that her son is going away to study in London and that her boyfriend has film jobs outside Bulgaria more and more often. They are where they are, and they swoop down on her from time to time. Things-as-it-is.

At 46, when loved ones leave, she can concentrate on herself or what's left of her. Because caring for others drives her life, when they leave she looks inside and sees a big gaping emptiness at home. The garden is overgrown with weeds, her role as mother has shielded her, torn her away from her responsibility to relate to herself. When those people jump on their horses and gallop off in all directions—one to study, the other to chase fame, yet a third to the beyond, then so much freedom pours down—freedom from her former roles and adrenaline that she'll gather speed, gather speed and take flight!

She no longer cares who ate what when, where he is, what he's doing, if they're OK, did she give him all the right coping strategies, did she give enough, whether she made a mistake, and so on. She's flying away into the unbearable lightness of being.

She wants to have everything that was put off. She wants it now, all at once. She wants to ride horses. She struggles with the horse over the soft hills, hangs out in pubs for hours just as she is, in breeches and riding boots covered with hay, and nobody calls to tell her to buy Coca-Cola or chocolate on the way home.

She runs into acquaintances from twenty years ago, straight out of Madame Tussauds.

She travels. Mends her faith in life.

She tries all sorts of methods for wellness and healthy eating, drags herself to massages, starts going to an Ayurvedic cooking class, draws, dances, writes.

She'll start singing. It's not that she doesn't get drunk on Corsican choirs and cry sweetly now and again. That's how her body feels the sorrow—sweetly, as her car moves through the soft hills outside the city like a May bumblebee. With the horses. For her, hugging them is the equivalent of hugging ten of her favorite creatures—such warmth and calm exude from their powerful necks. She isn't disgusted by the smell, or the blood when she splits her lip on the saddle, or the danger of subduing such a huge animal beneath her. Strength and calm afterward on the way back.

Such is the progression of the sharp decline of various functions, before others appear. The fear of emptiness, and of that which appears as it appears, is terrible. When she is afraid, her face in the mirror is old and dark. She doesn't like it and avoids looking at herself. She thinks of herself as ugly all day, except for when she accidentally catches sight of herself and realizes that it's not true.

She writes her fears on scraps of paper and sticks them up all over the house, so as to sanctify them regularly.

I am afraid:

That I am useless.

That they don't notice me anymore.

That if I'm not anyone's love interest and if I'm no longer of child-
bearing age

That I'm not important anymore.

That my lips will get pleated up like my mother's.

That everyone will leave me.

That there is nothing left.

Only silence and loneliness.

Who is afraid? the yoga teacher asks and laughs. *Who is the mother who is worried, who is worried? Ha ha ha!*

Very funny!

Her body does not want to eat like before. She thinks up new break-fasts.

Buckwheat Breakfast

```
Boil a handful of buckwheat. Add olive oil, lemon, and
salt to taste, finely chopped hot pepper, tomato. Improvise
according to the season—avocado, spinach leaves, bok
choy, grated green apple, or a spoonful of cream. This
breakfast is toning, filling, and easy to digest.
```

Oatmeal Breakfast

```
Mix a handful of finely ground oatmeal with a little
water and half a carton of yogurt. Add raw sunflower
seeds, almonds, hazelnuts, walnuts, and cashews. Add a
spoonful of ground flaxseeds and a spoonful of ground
sesame seeds. Add sliced fruit to taste and several dried
plums and raisins. This is an energy bomb that guarantees
long-lasting carbohydrates, vitamins, minerals, and
omega-3 fatty acids—important for building cells.
```

Her body also spits out her favorite clothes. She hosts a farewell party for her wardrobe. For two days she tries on all her clothes, remembering their straps, necklines, and bows, and all that she experienced while wearing them. She carefully packs them into paper bags. She writes her girlfriends' names on the bags. She looks at herself naked in the mirror—this shape needs different shapes. She buys champagne and fruit. She invites over her girlfriends—all young girls with amazing figures. They try on the clothes, strutting around in her feathers and romantic gowns. She watches them with envy, and joy. Her clothes will continue to cause thrills. Within a week, new shapes and colors appear. That which makes her life meaningful is to listen closely to the soul, to that buzzing within because:

Inside of me it's always 6:30 in the morning
When the day is blushing, and my skin
Promises inhalation
The blood moves in leaps

Through my watered-down innards
Always distracted and late
My ears already pick up
The whisper of scaly wings and
The tapping of a gigantic manicure on the sidewalk
But it's so noisy in the city

It's noisy like that

Deer

My son has left to study in England. Sorrow. I have not been separated from him for the last eighteen years. Every evening I beg the moon to tell my child how much I love him. I cry quietly in the dark by the window. I realize that he does not belong to me. Rupen has never belonged to me. This opens up an enormous emptiness. Love pours down in its place, made stronger by the fact that it cannot be shared. The guilt creeps out that I am not a sufficiently good mother. Fear as to whether my little birdie will fly the distance home.

Have more faith in being. It also loves your child, the Zen mentor Ganga said one day. *Children return to their mothers. Or perhaps they do not return. Existence takes care of them.*

I go into his room, sniff at T-shirts. Tears claw at my eyes when I see them on the streets in their low-slung pants and hoods, the same as he is: half-boys, half-men, their faces still delicate. I have the feeling that I'll run into him at any moment.

I begin collecting moments.

I live with that which I have: myself and the present.

I get up early and play tennis in the woods. I do new things. I learn to row. Alone on the lake, the slender tip of the boat cleaves the black water, the sun shines. It is so long and narrow that if I think about anything but the rowing or if I push too hard on one side, I'll get dunked immediately. All that can be heard is the soft slapping of the oars. The feeling of water, but I'm not wet. I press down, I let up. Press down, let up.

Red leaves fall. I look around for my life.

I wake up and immediately head for the mountain. I always walk along the river. It's drizzling slightly. I finally find a dusky place near the water between two slopes, make myself a bench of branches on top of a big stone and set the timer for twenty minutes. I let the river do its thing. When the tune rings out, I immediately turn it off and open my eyes. As always after meditation, the colors are intense. I notice the oak forest across the way, the light has changed. How did I not see all this before? I don't budge. I sit and look.

179

At that moment something living darts down the hill through the trees. A wolf. It flies straight at me. No. A deer. A young buck. Hardly able to contain his own strength, he leaps across the river and will swoop down on me a second later. I'm afraid to startle him for fear he might hurt me. I move slightly. He notices my gesture and changes his direction in midair. He crashes to the ground only two yards from the stone, freezes and looks at me. We stay like that for an eternity. Something different is looking at me from his eyes. After that he makes a small jump and looks at me again. He disappears with graceful leaps. For a long time I catch glimpses of his white lace panties in the loose-knit forest. I don't move. I sit. I sense that exactly at the moment when the animal appeared, I realized that the things that lie before me are Mine, my personal challenges, and they are waiting for me to answer them with all the passion and imagination I can muster. Until now, I've behaved rather nonchalantly towards my things. I resist, mull them over, drag my heels, grumble.

My good luck to stand in the path of the deer's pure intention to jump a river at that moment is a revelation. The forest gives me a lost key to my innermost self. His eyes, those yellowish-green eyes, are the same as mine. I look at myself with my own gaze. I am that deer, my drive, which frightens me. I've felt it, when the surf below me has started to take flight, barely tied to the water. I am seized by the same old terror that things are getting out of control and I always see catastrophic scenarios, in which I fall, get tangled up in the belt and can't swim up from beneath the sail. Exactly then, when the opportunity appears to expand beyond myself, the fear comes and seals me up.

The deer has disappeared. I sit on the stone, filled with his drive.

I think of the deer the next morning as I toss in bed. I obey my first impulse to get up and sense the freshness of the morning. It's drizzling. I jump into my rose boots and go out.

Calligraphy

In the beginning, we stand, drawing commas and bones for six hours at a stretch—the first steps in calligraphy. There are twenty or so of us; most of us came back from a Zen monastery last week, where we sat meditating in front of a wall all day. A terrifying fury comes out of me. FURY! Toward myself. Toward others. I thought I'd overcome it, but there's more. While I'm busy with the world, the weeds sprout up inside. Ganga—whom I've christened Yoda—wiggles her ears as she talks: "Don't push the anger down inside, because it'll sink and undermine you without you realizing it. Watch it gushing out. Watch it with compassion toward yourself."

Easier said than done. We're in complete silence. We have the right to speak only ten minutes a day—when puzzling out the koans Yoda gives us. When I make a mistake, she hits me ritually with her stick. Koans are paradoxical questions, an expression or action by the teacher, which reveal the essence of Zen consciousness. They are misleading, full of traps that rational thought falls into, to the point of stupefaction. Then a space for intuition and spontaneity opens up, in which the answer appears on its own. My latest koan: They asked Buddha: Does a dog have Buddha-nature? Buddha said: Everything has Buddha-nature. They asked the teacher Joshu: Does a dog have Buddha-nature? Joshu said: A dog does not have Buddha-nature. The question is: Who is right?

After spinning my wheels for one whole night, I see the answer. I can't tell it to you, so as not to deprive you of the opportunity to labor over it yourself, if you so desire. Yoda left me with that koan so I could observe its influence over my life.

She left me to observe my impulse to say who is right. To make pronouncements. To compare. To get caught up. To be dualistic. Fuck!

After the monastery, calligraphy is a soft paw on our souls, which are wounded from scrutiny.

We learn to mix the India ink with special smooth stones and take baby steps in drawing on bamboo in a house at the foot of the mountain. Sometimes Ganga or her long-haired Indian assistant come over to hold my arm, so I can feel how to enter and exit the bamboo leaf (the female) and how to close off the stalk (the male). I make distinct, strong stalks. One morning, Yoda says: "Forget everything, close your eyes and try to express yourself. Whatever comes to you. Whatever you feel. Paint from your belly."

I've just tightened up and am wondering how I'll scrape away all day over this flat leaf—yet another failure of my femininity—so permission to act outrageous is more than welcome. At first timidly, then more and more boldly, I spatter away with the fattest brushes.

My sheet is not enough for me. Winds blow, rains fall, which lash at the others' drawings as well. With each bespattered sheet I enter ever deeper into my belly and discover fury, pain and something dark roiling inside. At one point I open my eyes and see that the ink is almost gone. I take a new sheet. I grab the round stone tile and, inky as it is, stick it to the paper. I go to peel it off, but it doesn't budge; I pull with all my might and it slides a bit. I tear it away with an abrupt movement. That's it. I don't need to add anything more. I scribble several made-up hieroglyphs vertically to the side and run over to swipe one of Yoda's red stamps. I place it in the corner under the hieroglyphs with great satisfaction. The signature! Now the painting is finished. All of my tension is on the paper.

I go to the bathroom. My blood is flowing. What a privilege to paint my dislodging egg. I sit by the edge of the pool. I feel magnificent. Happy to coincide so much with that moment! Freedom!

I continue painting. I return to the bamboo and see that I am more expansive and braver. The others nearby sense it as well. They toss timid glances at my table. Inside the fear rises: perhaps I am setting myself apart too much, could my flight be showing? Yet the empty sheet calls me. I slice long and thin strips and look for objects. I feel like painting and don't give a shit about those around me. I wet the paper and without lifting the brush, I draw a clothespin. A really long clothespin. I hang the sheet on the line behind me and the pin drips. I start a series of clothespins. There is something about the shape that resembles a person. Something likeable in its usefulness and in the spring that moves it.

Thank God, today we don't have kundalini meditation as usual at the end, to shake off what happened during the day. Yoda sends us off to the mountain with a mysterious expression, telling us we should look at forms.

I head toward the Boyana Waterfall. Since I've started painting, I've been seeing better. I've gained a sense for detail—everything around is pictures. I look at the musculature of the trees: how they enter the ground or how they burst into space. Quiet. Such ones.

What has been created makes me shiver. I am slightly weightless without paper and brush. The fear begins to creep in, so what now? What more? How? Will I be able to?

I confide to the Indian that I am afraid of my boldness on that day, of my insatiability and pride. I desperately need this, yet I feel that it once again feeds the ego in some way. He laughs. "If the ego helps you bring out the creative within yourself—why not? Use it and enjoy it. When you enjoy that which you create, existence enjoys itself right along with you. The important thing is not to identify only with what has been done, to not take it as 'mine.'"

Later that evening, I randomly open *Zen Mind, Beginner's Mind* by Shunryu Suzuki:

> When we sit in the cross-legged posture, we resume our fundamental activity of creation. There are perhaps three kinds of creation. The first is to be aware of ourselves after we finish zazen.[8] When we sit we are nothing, we do not even realize what we are; we just sit. But when we stand up, we are there! That is the first step in creation. When you are there, everything else is there; everything is created all at once. When we emerge from nothing, when everything emerges from nothing, we see it all as a fresh new creation.
>
> This is non-attachment. The second kind of creation is when you act, or produce or prepare something like food or tea. The third kind is to create something within yourself, such as education, or culture, or art, or some system for our society. So there are three kinds of creation. But if you forget the first, the most important one, the other two will be like children who have lost their parents; their creation will mean nothing.
>
> Usually everyone forgets about zazen. Everyone forgets about God. They work very hard at the second and third kinds of creation, but God does not help the activity. How is it possible for Him to help when He does not realize who He is? That is why we have so many problems in this world ... But if we are aware that what we do or what we create is

---

[8] *za* means to sit, while *zazen* translates roughly as "sitting in a state of meditation," according to D.T. Suzuki.

really the gift of the "big I," then we will not be attached to it, and we will not create problems for ourselves or for others.

And we should forget, day by day, what we have done; this is true non-attachment. And we should do something new. To do something new, of course we must know our past, and this is all right. But we should not keep holding onto anything we have done; we should only reflect on it. And we must have some idea of what we should do in the future. But the future is the future, the past is the past; now we should work on something new. This is our attitude, and how we should live in this world. This is "dana prajna paramita," to give something, or to create something for ourselves. So to do something through and through is to resume our true activity of creation. This is why we sit. If we do not forget this point, everything will be carried on beautifully. But once we forget this point, the world will be filled with confusion.

I close the book.

I stand beyond these words . . .

Day after day, we mix the ink, dip our brushes in water, line up the sheets, get attuned to ourselves. We interrupt the painting from time to time to dance, meditate, eat, rest, or say what we have discovered about ourselves in what we are doing. Slightly bewildered, extracted from the intimacy with the paper, one after another we share what we have experienced along the way. Bella speaks softly. She's the wife of a rich man, with whom she signed up for the seminar. He is a middleman in finding various things for sale—a ship loaded with mazut, a tanker full of sugar, real estate in Mexico. He's strange; when you ask him something, he looks aside and never answers directly, if he answers at all. He looks at you with his fixed gaze for a moment, as if taking an instant photo, and says: *Hmm, yessss* . . . Bella is thin; her skin is tawny, contrasting with her blonde hair. She reminds me of a doe with those huge eyes. I have always taken her as his shadow. It's as if I'm seeing her for the first time in front of her paper. She paints delicately, attentively. She is beautiful . . . he comes over from time to time to watch her.

Bella says: "I've never done anything creative before. I'm trying it for the first time and I like it . . . Now I know this is what I want . . . and I'll do it."

There is calmness in her voice, submission to her desire and a certainty that she will surrender to it. She's enchanting, at once fragile and strong in her intention.

Tears fall from my eyes. Her words open some door within me. From there bursts a yearning for the freedom which creativity gives me, and pain that I live separated from its source. My tears turn into sobbing, into bawling, and when it is my turn to say how I'm doing with calligraphy today, I'm not in any condition to utter a word. I can barely contain all these emotions in the borders of my body, which has suddenly become terribly tight. I want to open my mouth and howl, to free my chest of this burden. But I'm ashamed. The observer within me coldly notes her amazement that I had missed being creative that much. The others are there—quiet, they wait through this sudden outburst. I attempt a few words, but my sobbing grows ever stronger. So I wave my hand and say in a single breath: "I can't . . . answer . . . right now . . ."

When the sharing ends, I go out and sit next to the water. The tears keep springing up—now quiet, unattached. I don't want to know.

I rub ink into the stone, a few drops of water; once again everyone in front of his table.

My painting is radically different. The bamboo leaves appear! Truly feminine, rounded, with delicate ends and beginnings. I surrender. I let the brush and the paper meet. I don't force out my intentions. I sniffle and sigh, freed from all that was cried out. My hand is soft. I enter the leaf carefully, let it round off and patiently exit, until its tip touches the nothingness.

Light. Water. Levity.

Drawing, too, like love, comes about through vulnerability.

Ganga's assistant passes by and surreptitiously gives my elbow an ecstatic squeeze.

The Zen parable comes to mind, in which a teacher has gone out begging with his student, but along the way they run across a deep river. While the teacher searches for a ford, the student splashes across the water and calls from the opposite bank: "Look, teacher! I can walk on water! Come on, you can do it, too!" The teacher looks at him and murmurs: "If I'd known you'd work miracles, I would've broken your legs."

Finale

I dream I'm playing the lead in some play. It will begin shortly, but I don't know my lines. I'm crawling on the floor, searching for them amidst the scattered sheets of paper. I put on dark-red velvet shoes with high sturdy heels, so as to better fit the role.

The curtain rises.

HER
All my life I've striven to be different.

HIM
You change the quality. You change it with your presence.
Nothing more is needed.